PUBLISHING

CORY MARTIN

LOVE LOCKS

Based on the Hallmark Hall of Fame Movie
Story by John Tinker and Neal Dobrofsky & Tippi Dobrofsky
Teleplay by Teena Booth and John Tinker

www.hallmarkpublishing.com
For more about the movie visit:
www.hallmarkmoviesandmysteries.com/love-locks

Chapter One

A Time and a Place

IN YOUNG LOVE, THERE ARE rarely specific dates. When you are in that all-consumed state, love has no number. Love is your first kiss in seventh grade outside the gym – sweaty palms, blue jeans, and curled hair. It is the boy who left you heartbroken the summer before senior year just as you made the varsity soccer team, and the wondering what happened to the guy you met on a family vacation to Hawaii.

Love is a marker of moments passing and standing still. It is a time and a place. And that is where this story begins...

Twenty years ago. Paris.

It was late fall, or early winter. The leaves were gone, but the sun still shone, and two Americans rode the streets on bicycles.

Lindsey and Jack met at the Sorbonne. She was an art student; he was a student of life with a major in business.

Lindsey had moved to the City of Lights in September to study art at the university as an exchange student. Jack, though an American, had lived in Europe for most of his life. His father, a hotelier and restaurateur, showed Jack the world through his businesses. While Jack was studying the economy in class, he was learning it firsthand at his father's latest hotel in Paris.

Though it may have seemed as if they came from two separate worlds, they were more similar than many would believe. They both worked hard—she at painting, he at pleasing his father. Jack had plans to own his own hotel one day. Each had dreams of the future where life was grand, yet they also understood the importance of the moment. As twenty-somethings, they lived young and carefree.

The contents of their bike baskets jiggled along the cobblestone streets. The colors in her paint box shook with every pedal stroke, and the baguette peeking out of his picnic basket bobbed up and down. They spent many days on their bikes, weaving in and out of the hidden parts of Paris.

"Let's stop here," Jack said as they approached the Place Du Tertre, a square at the heart of the Montmartre quarter where a penniless Picasso had once lived. Lindsey happily obliged. It was one of her favorite places to paint.

She appreciated small ways Jack supported her, like this—choosing to picnic in a spot she loved. He understood her, despite not being an artist himself.

As they leaned their bikes against a lamppost and locked them up, Jack pointed to a man painting portraits with a cat beside him.

"We should get one done," Jack said.

"A portrait? Really?" She viewed this kind of painting as a cheesy tourist attraction meant to sucker men into buying things for women. Plus, where would they hang it? His place or hers?

"It'll be fun." Jack grabbed her hand and gently guided her toward the man's easel. "You need something to remember Paris by once you go back to New York."

"But I'll have you." Lindsey didn't need a generic painting to remember her time with Jack.

"How much?" Jack asked the artist.

The artist looked at them. "Thirty francs, but if you hold my cat, I give you a discount."

How could she say no to a man and his cat? She looked at Jack and smiled, then turned to the artist. "We'll do it."

Jack handed the man the money and pulled his red knit hat off his head. Lindsey fluffed his brown hair to make him present-able, then grabbed the gray-and-white cat and placed it between them as they sat close on a small chair. Jack leaned over and kissed her windblown cheek.

"That kiss. That is, what do you call it? The... the... essence of the two of you. That is what I shall capture." The artist made round-ed strokes as though sketching the shapes of their heads in black charcoal against a pre-painted backdrop of the Eiffel Tower.

Though she knew the painting wouldn't end up in a museum one day, Lindsey felt her heart lift with happiness. She reached over and squeezed Jack's hand. This moment she would remember forever, regardless of whether the sketch captured anything at all. It would be a reminder that life could never be fully planned. If she'd arranged every detail of the day, they wouldn't be getting a painting done right now.

Lindsey had come to Paris to learn how to paint, not with technical skills but with the kind of passion she felt every time she entered the Louvre. She hadn't come to fall in love or find "the one." She was young and looking to a future where she might one day have her pieces hanging in a gallery. She'd come to Paris with a mission. Nobody would interrupt her process. She was strictly there to perfect her craft. However, the first time she'd seen Jack's blue eyes, she'd known she was in trouble.

After the first two weeks with Jack, her vision of the future had changed. And now, she couldn't imagine life without him.

Her time at the Sorbonne was nearly over, and she and Jack had discussed their future. After he finished school, he would come to New York. She needed to know what it would be like if he was part of her world— not in this fairytale land, as Paris often felt like to her, but New York City. She knew everything about him, and she wanted Jack to see the other part of her world.

A small piece of her feared that, like all great things in life, their relationship would eventually come to an end, but another part looked excitedly toward the future. For now, she was content that they would have this sketch to remind them of their time together in Paris.

"Should I be smiling or should I be brooding?" Jack asked, interrupting Lindsey's train of thought.

"Smile, of course," Lindsey said. "I love your smile."

"This one?" Jack grinned as wide as he could. He looked cartoonish. Lindsey giggled.

The artist interrupted their moment of playfulness. "Um, no, *monsieur*. My cat is

Cheshire cat. You? Please, smile like a young man."

Lindsey and Jack burst out laughing, then looked at each other and turned to the artist with the biggest grins they could each muster.

The artist shook his head, then continued painting. Ten minutes later, he finished the piece.

"Okay, lovebirds. I am done. You take this and enjoy your day together. And you," he said as he turned to Jack, "don't forget—a woman that you can make smile like that is a woman you keep." Jack's face suddenly became serious as the artist handed him the finished painting. For just a moment, Lindsey thought she caught a bit of fear in his eyes.

No. She was imagining things, perhaps because of her own fears about whether their connection would last.

Lindsey took the painting from Jack's hands and studied it. Their faces were nearly caricature-like, and the background with the Eiffel Tower was terrifically touristy, but Lindsey loved it. "It's beautiful," she said and thanked him for his work.

"Maybe I see you two again sometime," the artist said.

"Maybe," Lindsey whispered as they walked off.

As Jack unlocked the bikes, Lindsey

stopped him. "Why'd you get so serious back there?"

"What do you mean? I did?" Jack sounded defensive.

Lindsey paused. Maybe she shouldn't ask the question on her mind. But she had to know. "Are you sure that guy didn't freak you out when he mentioned you should keep me?"

"What? That's crazy. Of course I'm going to keep you," Jack said. "So are we heading to the bridge now?"

Lindsey nodded. Today was supposed to be a special day for them.

The tradition in Paris was that couples would write their names on a lock, place it on the metal grates of the Pont des Arts—a pedestrian bridge that connected the Instuit de France and the Palais du Louvre —and throw away the key. The bridge was the first metal thruway constructed in the city. Engineers had conceived it to resemble a suspended garden. It had become home to the fate of thousands of couples worldwide.

Lindsey and Jack planned to seal their fate on the very same bridge.

As they rode past Notre Dame Cathedral and the Louvre, she thought about the past three months. During that time, she and Jack had spent every moment—when she wasn't painting or he wasn't working with his dad—together. Outside of class, they were inseparable. Today would be their day to declare their devotion to one another.

They rode side by side through the city streets, then out to the river, and stopped halfway across the bridge. They hopped off their bikes and stood at the railing covered in locks. Lindsey placed her hand over the lock in her pocket. She'd bought it two days ago at the local hardware store before she'd even had the courage to ask Jack if he would put a lock on the bridge with her. Yesterday, she'd asked him if he would do it and he'd happily agreed. Putting the lock on the bridge was the only thing Lindsey had planned for the day, and, she supposed, for their future. After all, that's what the lock symbolized—a love that could not be broken.

Lindsey looked at Jack's blue eyes and immediately became lost. The cool winter breeze nipped at her ears, and the crisp smell of the water from the Seine whipped by her nose. In the distance, she could see the tip-top of the Eiffel Tower. All around them, couples were fastening their locks to the bridge. Her heart ached. Moments like these made her never want to leave Paris.

"I don't want to go back to New York," she said, and then had an idea. "What if I don't? I can stay here and paint."

"Hey, we have a plan, right?" He grabbed

her hand and pulled her close with a smile. "It's going to be fine."

Lindsey knew they would see each other again soon, but still, she wasn't ready to leave. "It feels like we're saying goodbye."

"It's not goodbye. It's a few months," Jack said, but Lindsey knew it wasn't that simple.

"Did you tell your father you're quitting?"

Jack's part of the plan was to quit working for his father, go to New York, and find a job there, but he'd been putting off the first step for weeks. "I will." He put his arms around Lindsey. "We'll be back together by Valentine's Day."

The thought of being back with Jack on the most romantic day of the year made everything seem okay. "Top of the Empire State Building?" Lindsey asked.

"Not quite the top of the Eiffel Tower, but it'll do," Jack answered as he took Lindsey in his arms and kissed her. The only time she had ever been to the top of the Eiffel Tower was with Jack. It was there they had shared their first kiss. She imagined that their first kiss in the States would be at the top of the Empire State Building. That way, each moment their lips met on different soil would always have a special time and a place.

She lingered in their embrace for a moment longer before gently pulling away. Lindsey took the lock from her left pocket and produced a Sharpie marker from the right. She held up the lock proudly, then wrote her name on it.

"We lock it on the bridge, and our love will last forever," she said as she handed the lock to Jack.

"Forever?" Jack said with a slight inflection as if he were asking a question. Lindsey tried to ignore it as he wrote his name. Jack held up the lock. "With this lock, I thee..."

It slipped in his gloved hands. She reached for it, but as she put her hand out, it went flying. They both scrambled to catch it, but it was no use. They watched as the symbol of their love went sailing through the air and over the railing, falling into the water with a loud splash.

Jack's mouth fell open. Lindsey gasped.

"You dropped it on purpose!" she exclaimed.

"No, no. That was your fault. You grabbed for it."

She fought to rise above her bewilderment and hurt. Maybe neither of them was to blame... or maybe they both were. Anyway, what was the point in arguing? It was done. They looked down in silence at the water, where the lock had sunk and disappeared forever.

Three weeks later, Lindsey returned to New York. Jack remained in Paris.

She sometimes thought of the lock rusting at the bottom of the Seine. The water would lap against their names until they were no longer recognizable.

For years, she thought of him, but learned to move on.

They never celebrated Valentine's Day or shared their first kiss on American soil at the top of the Empire State Building.

In fact, as time passed, Lindsey believed they'd never kiss again. She let the thought of a future with Jack disappear, just as their lock had done that day.

Their love would remain in the past—a time and a place long forgotten.

Chapter Two

New York

WHEN THE MINUTIAE OF LIFE take over, the time and the place are no longer signifiers of love: they simply are. Dates, hours, minutes turn into markers of meetings, deadlines, to-do lists. Time moves at an unthinkable pace. Numbers become a driving force. Seasons change. One year morphs into the next.

That is where the story begins yet again.

Dead of winter. New York City. Twenty years later.

Lindsey took the tall drip from the barista at the kiosk on the corner of East Forty-Second into her leather-gloved hands. "Thanks, Mario," she said as she dropped a dollar into the tip jar.

"You're welcome," Mario said. "It's a pleasure to see you every morning."

"You, too. See you tomorrow!"

Mario waved as she walked off into the

bustling crowds. The lightly falling snow dusted the top of her head. She'd pulled her blonde hair back into a ponytail, leaving her ears cold. Lindsey's brisk pace kept the rest of her warm, though, as she trudged through the slush that had gathered along the sidewalks. Her tall boots and black trench coat were practical but also stylish, perfect for the quintessential New York businesswoman.

Lindsey was the founder and editor in chief of *POV*, a notable magazine. Though its circulation was small compared to the well-established art glossies, *POV* had found its niche and a strong following. She was proud of the periodical. Next to her daughter, it was her everything. Even if it wasn't what she'd set out to do with her life, she felt that she'd managed to make a career out of her knowledge of art.

The office was already bustling with art directors, copy editors, and writers pulling together the latest issue. Standing desks with large computers were organized in rows. It was a sleek but creative environment.

"Morning, Lindsey," her assistant said as Lindsey made her way through *POV*.

"Morning, Maggie." Lindsey continued walking toward her office.

Maggie fell into step with her. She looked sharp as always in a suit with a red blouse that complimented her dark skin. "First cup of coffee?"

"Third. We set for the Valentine's Day issue?" It was the beginning of January, and the magazine had to go to print in a few days.

"You just need to pick a cover." Maggie held up her iPad and flipped through two different options. One was all red with simple graphics and the other showed a Cupid with a heart and arrow.

"Not the Cupid." Lindsey hadn't been a fan of Valentine's Day for quite some time now, and the Cupid was too much. "The last thing I want to think about is a chubby toddler coming at me with a weapon."

"Such a romantic," Maggie quipped. Lindsey laughed and refrained from making an even more cynical comment. Maybe Maggie still had a sense of naiveté when it came to love. Though Lindsey's own idea of love as magic had gone, she didn't want to ruin it for someone else. Especially Maggie, who'd been her rock the past couple years as the magazine had grown. If she still believed in romance, then Lindsey didn't want to stop her. "Oh, speaking of romance," Maggie said, "Trent Greer's in your office."

"What?" Trent Greer owned several of the biggest magazines in the world. He also happened to be one of the most eligible bachelors in the city. He was smart, successful, and good-looking. He'd never been married and had hit the perfect age of bachelorhood—forty-six. He'd established his career, owned a home—probably several—knew what he wanted, and simply needed the perfect woman to complement his lifestyle. Just about everyone knew who he was. "What does he want?"

"Who cares? He's gorgeous." Maggie handed Lindsey a document. Behind her glasses, her eyes narrowed. "Before you go in there, do something with your hair."

Lindsey took a quick glance at her reflection in the glass. She was perfectly put together. "What's wrong with my hair?"

Maggie shrugged. "You could try wearing it down sometime," she said lightly.

"Don't you have something to do?" Lindsey teased. Maggie laughed as she walked away.

I look fine, Lindsey thought. I'm going into an unexpected meeting with a peer, and I look completely acceptable.

Lindsey stepped into her office: a large, spare space with a huge window overlooking the city. Trent was dressed in a navy pinstriped suit, most likely bespoke, made specifically for his taut body. He stood tall and confident as Lindsey walked in.

"Trent, what a surprise." Lindsey tried not to stare too long. She had seen him at gallery openings around the city, but they'd never conversed much nor been this close in person.

"I hope this is a good surprise," he said with a flash of his perfect white teeth.

"It's good." Lindsey thought about the fact that she hadn't been on a date in over a year, then quickly stopped herself. She was in her office, and Trent was probably there because of business.

"Good. Good." An awkward pause hung between them. "I'm glad. I wanted to catch you before you left. Your assistant said you're leaving for Paris with your daughter tomorrow."

Her daughter, Alexa, was eighteen and had completed her first semester at the University of Connecticut. Saying goodbye to Alexa the past August had been hard. Lindsey hadn't been alone in a long while. After Jack, she'd spent one year single, then met Dane. She'd been eager to believe she'd found love again, and before long, they'd gotten married. A year later, Alexa had been born. She and Dane had divorced when Alexa was two.

Alexa had lived with Lindsey most of the time, so the past four months of living alone in her Brooklyn loft had been an adjustment, to say the least. Now Alexa was going to study in France. Although the art program at UConn was one of the best in the state, it wasn't the same as the Sorbonne. That's why Alexa had applied to the same exchange program Lindsey had gone on. Though Lindsey was dreading taking her daughter to Paris, she was also happy for her.

"Did my assistant also tell you what I ate for breakfast?" Lindsey asked, teasing.

"French toast?" Trent responded. They both laughed. It was a moment Lindsey hadn't had in a while. She imagined suggesting to him that they meet for breakfast sometime, or dinner... but no. He wasn't here for romance.

"I can't believe you're old enough to have a daughter old enough to be in college," Trent said.

"Well, I *am* old enough to know when someone's buttering me up," Lindsey quipped.

"All right, here it is. I'd like to take you out."

Lindsey paused. Her thoughts of dating him were just fantasy, the kind people had about George Clooney or Brad Pitt. The what-if thoughts that are never supposed to come true. "Oh," she said.

"And I'd like to buy your magazine."

Now things were starting to make a little more sense. This wasn't really about her—it was about her business.

"Oh," she said again.

Trent looked perplexed. "Is that a yes/yes, no/yes, or yes/no?"

Lindsey paused. Now she was the one confused. "Yes. And no. I don't know."

Trent smiled and straightened his tie. "You've done an incredible job with *POV*. It's unique and you've done it yourself on a limited budget. I've been watching you for a while now."

"You have?" She knew he knew her name, but other than that, it was odd that he'd done his research. She understood now what was happening. Him asking her out wasn't about her single status, it was about her magazine's status. "I'm flattered."

"You should be. You've done amazing things with *POV*. But here's the thing—your readership's maxed out."

Now Lindsey could feel herself getting defensive. She had poured everything into *POV*. Though she'd wanted more kids, things hadn't worked out that way, and her magazine had become her second child. When she and Dane had divorced three years into their marriage, she'd quit painting altogether. At that point, it had become a luxury. It was no longer a passion that she hoped would turn into a career. Hope didn't pay the bills, and neither did her art.

Lindsey had gone to work consulting for galleries around New York City. When Alexa was in second grade, Lindsey had started *POV* out of the small Queens apartment she'd been able to afford with her consulting work and the alimony Dane paid. Year after year, the magazine had grown, and by the time Alexa entered high school, Lindsey was able to afford a staff and offices in a prime high-rise.

Yes, their readership was still too low, but she had plans to grow it. She didn't want to sell the magazine now.

"We're doing fine with the readers we have," Lindsey said.

"True. But you could be doing better. I can help you take *POV* to the next level."

Lindsey had been in business long enough to know that when someone wanted to help you take things to the next level, it almost always meant something else. He wasn't there to give her guidance and help.

"You want to buy me out?"

"You'll stay on to consult," Trent said with a smile, as if he'd just offered her the keys to the kingdom.

"So I'd be working for you then."

"No, you'd be working *with* me." Trent moved a little closer. "That wouldn't be so bad, would it?"

"The thing is, I'm pretty used to being my own boss," Lindsey said. This was true. She hadn't worked for anyone else in over ten years. The thought of working under someone, even if he was one of the hottest guys in publishing, sounded like instant death to her. She'd already given up once on her dreams. She wasn't about to give this up, too.

"Believe me, I get that. When I opened my first publishing house, the last thing on my mind was selling it. But I did. And I ended up building a bigger one," Trent said.

He had a point. But still, she wasn't ready to let go so quickly.

"Just think about it while you're away," he said. "And the other 'it,' too. I really would like to take you out."

"I will. And I will," Lindsey replied, more confused than ever.

Trent's phone rang. He hit ignore then turned to her. "Almost forgot, I'm in London next week. It's a short flight to Paris. I could show you our offices there."

"You must really want this magazine."

"That, too," he replied as he picked up his phone and dialed the last caller. "See you soon," he said as he left her office.

Lindsey stood in silence and watched as Trent disappeared around the corner. What had just happened?

"Tell me he's not the best-looking guy you've ever seen," Maggie said as she walked into the doorway and caught the tail end of Trent leaving.

"I wish I could," Lindsey said, deadpan.

Maggie turned to look at her. "What's wrong?"

"He wants to buy the magazine." Saying those words out loud suddenly made the whole exchange seem hyper-real.

"Seriously?" Maggie asked. Lindsey nodded. "What did you say?"

"I wanted to say 'no,' but somehow, I didn't. I'm not even sure what I said."

"I'm pretty sure he has that effect on everyone," Maggie said. They both smiled because it was true. For a moment, they were silent, and then Maggie asked, "Would it be so bad to sell? I'm leaving in a few months anyway." She'd gotten an offer to be an editor at a magazine based in Los Angeles, and Lindsey had understood why she couldn't refuse. While Maggie loved New York, she also loved the water and the lack of seasons on the West Coast.

"That's exactly why I can't sell. You're leaving. My daughter's leaving. I'm not giving up my business, too." The reality of the situation hit Lindsey hard. What would she do without *POV*? She'd have nothing.

"Are you sure you don't want to sell? He is *soooo* good-looking. Getting to stare at him every day might be worth it."

Lindsey laughed at Maggie's comment.

"I thought that might get you," Maggie said.

Lindsey smiled, then realized she didn't have to figure everything out in that moment. "C'mon, let's finish the layout. We have to get the February issue out today." Together, Lindsey and Maggie walked over to one of the designer's desks. The interior design of one of the pages was pulled up on the screen.

A painting with white titles over it was on the left side of the page. "Increase the opacity so we can see the titles better, move the Gaucher to center, and make it five by seven so it almost touches the borders," Lindsey said. The graphic artist made the changes with a few clicks on her keyboard. "Perfect," Lindsey said. "Send the final files in. We're ready to print."

Maggie and Lindsey walked away and headed back toward Lindsey's office. "You packed yet?" Maggie asked.

"I'm packing tonight." Lindsey had been putting it off. She still couldn't believe her daughter was moving so far away or that she was going back to Paris after all these years. She hadn't returned since she'd studied abroad. Valentine's Day that year had come and gone, and Jack never arrived. The phone calls and letters slowed to a halt, and honestly, she'd all but forgotten about him—until her daughter had decided to spend the next semester following in her footsteps.

"Throw in something sexy," Maggie said with a smile.

"Why?" Lindsey was going to be spending every day and night with her daughter before she moved into her dorm.

"You're going to Paris, girl. Not New Jersey."

Maggie did have a point, but Lindsey didn't want to think about it. The last time she fell in love in Paris, she'd ended up heartbroken.

She had no plans to repeat her past. This trip to France would be all about Alexa. Speaking of, she still had a lot to do before she left, and her daughter would be home soon. She smiled and finished the last of her coffee. "You know what? I'm going to take the rest of the day off. Can you handle everything? The next issue's ready for print, and I do need to pack."

"Of course," Maggie said.

"I'll be on my cell if you need me," Lindsey said, then left the office.

Back home in Brooklyn, Lindsey finished putting the last of her clothes into her suitcase. She crammed four days' worth of sightseeing outfits, including shoes, into one small suitcase. Just before she zipped up the bag, she paused and thought about what Maggie had said. *Throw in something sexy.*

She went back into her closet and pulled out a little black dress that she'd last worn to the *POV* launch party years ago. She'd purchased the classic designer dress with the first order of the magazine. She'd been wary about spending that much money before the magazine had launched, but now she half-believed that the dress had brought her luck. She could at least take along a little luck. She'd need it to get through saying goodbye to Alexa for so long without a bunch of tears. As she folded up the dress, something in the back of her closet caught her eye.

She reached inside and pulled out a painting of a beautiful Paris scene. It was the last full painting she'd done when she was abroad. It had always hung in her apartment, but when she'd moved to her loft in Brooklyn three years ago, she'd placed it in the back of the closet. She'd held on to the painting as a reminder that there was a time and a place when life was simple and full of love. Now that she was approaching forty, and the magazine had grown, *and* she'd been able to purchase her own home, she felt like life was good. She didn't need a reminder of her younger years anymore. But holding that painting in her hands brought back a flood of memories.

What had happened to Jack? She'd never bothered to ask her mentor, Hugo, because he would've tracked Jack down and demanded answers. Even if Jack had a good explanation, the answers wouldn't have changed a thing. The fact was, Jack never showed up. He'd made his choice clear. He didn't want to spend his life with her. But now that she was going back to Paris, she couldn't help but wonder where he'd ended up. Was he still there, or had his father taken him to another city to work on his latest hotel?

Lindsey picked up the painting and was about to put it back in the closet when a voice came from around the corner.

"Hi, Mom!"

Lindsey nearly dropped the painting as Alexa came bounding into her bedroom.

"You're early!" Lindsey leaned the painting against the wall and gave her daughter a giant hug. Then she looked her over, wondering if she'd been eating right and getting enough sleep. She looked healthy and cheerful, her long brown hair pulled back from her face.

"I caught a ride from a guy at school," Alexa said.

"What guy?" Lindsey asked with a sense of worry.

"I found him on the ride board in the dorm." Alexa looked pleased with herself.

"You drove from Connecticut with a total stranger?" It seemed as if just yesterday Alexa was waiting for the bus to take her to kindergarten. Now she was driving home from college—with a stranger.

"I was with two other friends, Mom. It's no big deal."

"So *all three* of you rode with a total stranger," Lindsey said, pointing out the obvious.

"Mom... you're helicoptering again."

Lindsey thought for a moment. "You're right. Engine's off." Her daughter was about to live in Paris—she could handle herself. But still, she couldn't help but worry.

"Hey, I remember that," Alexa said as she picked up the painting. "It used to be in the hallway at our old place. It was one of my favorites growing up. You should put it up again."

"We have better taste now," Lindsey said as she took the painting and put it back in the closet behind a couple of umbrellas and some old coats.

Alexa reached for it again. "You know, that painting is one of the reasons I'm going to Paris now."

Lindsey stopped her. "You're going to the Sorbonne. That's why you're going. It's an education and an experience that you can't miss."

"Yes, but I never would've known about the Sorbonne had I not asked you all those questions every time I passed that painting when I was little."

Alexa had a point. Lindsey smiled at the memory. Her daughter had constantly wanted to hear more about her life as a painter, even if it was a small blip in the big scheme of things.

Lindsey pulled Alexa in for another hug. "You always were a curious one."

"I was. So, tell me again, why did you stop painting?"

"I guess my fine arts degree taught me the fine art of unemployment," Lindsey replied so quickly that even she believed it was true. Yes, there was truth to that statement, but there was so much more.

After that day on the bridge with Jack, she'd stopped painting. She hadn't told anyone that at the time. Instead, she'd pretended that she was working on projects secretly. But it wasn't true. Her plan was to start painting again in New York, but when he never came, she'd lost interest. Then it became easy to blame it on lack of time. She was newly married, and then had a baby, then needed money to support herself and Alexa. Although it had been her first love, painting had become the thing that evoked the most regret.

"Maybe you'll start again," Alexa said.

"It's your turn now, kiddo," Lindsey said in all honesty. Her time had passed. Now was Alexa's time to experience the magic of youth. "You hungry?"

Alexa nodded and in unison, they said, "Pasta. Alfredo sauce. Extra cheese." It was a ritual for the two of them. Whenever they wanted to connect or life seemed to get too serious, they always had Alfredo pasta.

Lindsey missed having her baby at home. Yes, in her mind, Alexa would always be the little girl curled up in her arms late at night in their small Queens apartment. Alexa, whether she knew it or not, had been through some of the tough times of Lindsey's life. In some ways, Alexa was like Lindsey's guardian angel.

"I can't wait for you to meet Hugo," Lindsey said as she stirred the simmering sauce.

"Me either!" For years, Lindsey had told Alexa stories about Hugo. Even though Alexa had never met him, she seemed to consider him as some kind of uncle. When she was accepted into the exchange program, the first thing she inquired about was Hugo. She wanted to mentor under him just as her mom had done.

"He's the best teacher. He's kind of a meddler, so don't let him know anything about your social life," Lindsey said. When she and Jack first started dating, Hugo needed to know all the details. He wanted to know where Jack was from, how they met, and most important, if they felt the *amour*. Lindsey had made the mistake of telling him they were indeed in love, and he was the one who had encouraged her to prompt Jack to put a lock on the bridge. At the time, she was painting a scene of the bridge and the locks, and Hugo had told her that paintings have more meaning when you experience them in real life. His advice was similar to the words of wisdom writers had been receiving for years.

"Paint what you know," Hugo had said.

Lindsey loved the scene she had painted on the bridge, but she knew it was missing that *je ne sais quoi*. So, she had tried to experience the power of the locks. To her dismay, she was never able to complete the painting, because as hard as she tried, it never felt quite right. She'd left the unfinished canvas behind and completely forgotten about it until that moment.

Lindsey shook her head to release the memory and went back to making the pasta and focusing on Alexa.

"Though, I wouldn't worry about Hugo meddling too much. I don't expect you to have much of a social life because you'll be busy studying and painting, right?" Lindsey prodded, hoping that her daughter didn't feel the need to experience life in France the way she had.

"Yes, Mom," Alexa said as she picked up *The New York Times* crossword puzzle from the kitchen table. "Ten letter word for soul mate?"

"Delusional?"

Alexa shook her head. "You're terrible."

"Or realistic. Why should there be only one person for everyone?" Lindsey asked. After Jack and then Dane, she no longer believed in "the one."

"But what if there is?" Alexa asked. "What if there is just one person?"

As a mom, Lindsey wanted to keep her daughter's hope and innocence alive, but as a woman who'd experienced love and loss, she wanted to stop her daughter from making the same mistakes she had. "Remember when I had to tell you there was no Tooth Fairy? Well... brace yourself again," Lindsey said.

"Just because you were right about the Tooth Fairy, doesn't mean you're right about this."

Lindsey shook her head. She wanted to explain further, but there was no use arguing. She was Alexa's age once, and she knew how hopelessly romantic a young girl could be.

Alexa's phone started buzzing and she looked down at the screen. "It's Dad."

"Right on time. Proof positive that love is like the Tooth Fairy."

"Mom!" Alexa exclaimed as she picked up the phone. She started talking to her dad.

Lindsey went back to cooking, but she could overhear Dane tell Alexa to be careful.

While he hadn't been a great husband, he'd always been a great father, and for that, Lindsey was appreciative.

"Say hi to Jane for me," Alexa said before hanging up.

"Who's Jane?" Lindsey asked.

"Dad and Marcie are separated. It looks like he's headed for number three."

"I'm sorry to hear that," Lindsey said, and she meant it. Marcie and Dane married two years after his and Lindsey's divorce. Although things were complicated at first, Lindsey knew that Alexa and Marcie had a good relationship, and she hated to see her daughter have to deal with more disruption of family than she already had, even if she was an adult. "You shouldn't refer to your dad's wives by number."

"At least you're still number one."

"Yay," Lindsey said apathetically.

"You know what I look forward to? The day I get to tell Dad that you're with someone else," Alexa quipped. Since the split, Lindsey had dated men here and there, but she'd never found anyone serious. For her, love was never a focus. She already had her two loves—Alexa and the magazine. She didn't have time for anything else.

"At least you'll always have something to look forward to," Lindsey said.

"Mom. Come on. I'm in college now. You have this whole giant place to yourself. Don't you want someone to share it with?"

"I get to share it with you during holidays and summer. Besides, I'm more concerned with work right now," Lindsey said.

"You always say that," Alexa said.

"Actually, someone wants to buy *POV*. And not just someone—Trent Greer."

Alexa's eyes lit up. "The publishing guy?" Lindsey nodded. "That's great!"

"It would be if I was selling," Lindsey replied.

"Would that be so bad?"

"Sweetie, it's what I do every day. It's who I am. I'm not selling my life."

Alexa looked as if she was going to hold back, but couldn't stop herself from saying more. "What life? All you do is work. You know I love the magazine, but it's the only relationship you have."

"I have you," Lindsey protested.

"When was the last time you went out

and did something that wasn't related to business?"

Lindsey thought about it for a moment. There had to be something else she did, but she couldn't think of anything. She tried again, but nothing. Finally, she decided to change the subject.

"Can you believe you're going to Paris for three whole months?" she asked.

"Nice pivot." Her daughter knew when she was deflecting.

"Helicopters pivot, right?" Lindsey asked. She didn't want to talk about letting go of *POV* anymore.

"You know what? You're right. I can't believe I'll be in Paris for three months. I'm excited. Are you?" Alexa asked.

"For you? Absolutely."

"I meant for you, Mom. You haven't been to Paris in twenty years. I'm sure it's going to be amazing."

"I'm sure it will be," Lindsey replied.

"We're going to have fun. We're going to Paris!"

Lindsey smiled at Alexa's enthusiasm then pulled the pot of boiling water off the stove. She fished out two noodles, handed one to Alexa, then grabbed one for herself. Together, they threw them against the wall. The pasta stuck and they exclaimed, "Done!"

"Now let's eat. We've got an early flight to

catch, and you need your beauty rest," Alexa said.

"Excuse me?" Lindsey asked with a smile.

"No offense, Mom. But you're not as young as you used to be, and you never know who you might meet. It's Paris! Anything can happen."

Isn't that right, Lindsey thought, then wondered once again what had happened to Jack.

Chapter Three

Paris

FROM TEN THOUSAND FEET, LINDSEY could almost smell the fresh croissants of her favorite bakery near the Sorbonne. Even two decades later, her mouth still watered at the memory. She made a mental note to stop for one when she took Alexa to sign up for classes. She hoped they'd still be around, but then she remembered that the establishments of Paris, unlike the relationships formed there, lasted forever—or so it seemed—and she probably had nothing to worry about.

"Are we there yet?" Alexa asked groggily as she woke and stretched in her seat.

"Twenty minutes," Lindsey replied. "Are you ready?"

"I will be once I have a coffee. Speaking of, how many have you had? Did you not sleep at all?"

Lindsey had spent the entire eight-hour flight online, researching Trent Greer and his company. To sell or not to sell? That was the question. "I slept," she said, completely lying.

"Doesn't look like it."

"Hey," Lindsey said. "Give me a tooth-brush, some eyeliner, and a fresh coat of lip gloss, and I'll be looking just fine in five minutes."

"You do know it's ten in the morning here, right? You probably should've slept."

"I'll be fine," Lindsey said with a yawn. "I promise."

She took a deep breath to wake herself. This was Paris, and Alexa didn't want to spend the whole time in the hotel room. But Lindsey would be fine. At work, she'd been known to pull all-nighters, and she func-tioned well on little sleep.

Alexa looked out the window as they approached the City of Lights. She squeezed her mom's hand. "We're almost there!"

Lindsey smiled. It was good to see Alexa so happy.

The plane began its descent, and twenty minutes later, it landed at Charles de Gaulle Airport. Soon after, they had their bags and were seated in the back of a Mercedes-Benz taxi headed straight for the city.

Alexa stared out the window, bright-eyed. Lindsey watched the way her face lit up. It reminded her of when Alexa was young. Every time she passed by her painting in their Queens apartment, she'd ask Lindsey about the Sorbonne and Paris. Lindsey would have to regale Alexa with another tale, another memory, a description of the famous sights. Now that they were heading to Paris for Alexa, the tables had turned. Alexa was the one spouting everything she knew about the city. When they were in flight, Alexa had showed Lindsey a notebook full of research. She had a list of the quaint cafés they had to go to, and notes of the best walks to take. Alexa had explained that she'd read article after article and scoured social media to learn the best times to visit the most popular and iconic sights. She had everything planned.

Alexa pointed over her mother's shoulder. "Mom, look. It's the Eiffel Tower. We need to go!"

Well, that one was on every visitor's list. Lindsey smiled. Alexa's enthusiasm was contagious.

"We'll go," Lindsey said as she took in the massive metal structure. It was every bit the same as she'd remembered—spectacular, full of promise, and daunting all at once.

"Have you been to the top?" Alexa asked.

"Only once." Jack had planned an entire day for them around the tower. First, there was a picnic in the park, then there were cappuccinos from the barista with the white-and-black striped shirt, and finally, at sunset, there was the ride to the top. At the pinnacle of the landmark, they'd shared their first kiss... the gentlest, most skin-tingling kiss she'd ever experienced. Lindsey could still remember the blood-orange color of the sky that night. She'd spent weeks afterward trying to replicate the exact shade for her final painting, but never could get it right. Then the lock had dropped into the Seine, and Lindsey had returned to New York City. The painting remained unfinished.

"I can't believe you never came back," Alexa mused. Her gaze was still focused on the world outside her window.

"Well, now I'm back. This time with my girl." Lindsey grabbed Alexa's hand and squeezed it tight. The cabdriver merged into the traffic flowing past the Eiffel Tower, and the sight slowly disappeared behind them.

Ten minutes later, they arrived at the Hôtel Pierre Du Calvet. It was a small hotel, quaint yet luxurious, located on a side street paved in cobblestones. The exterior was covered in a rich, dark wood with burgundy awnings above the entrance.

"I guess this is us," Lindsey said as they emerged from the cab, taking it all in.

"It *is* us. It's perfect," Alexa said, and Lindsey agreed. The hotel looked like the kind of place you read about in novels where luminaries of years past met for drinks to discuss grand ideas.

"Of course it's perfect. Hugo recommended it," Lindsey said with a smile. Even though she hadn't yet seen him, she could already feel Hugo's presence.

"I like him already," Alexa said as she walked around the car to the hotel. She looked ready to say more when she looked up and found herself face-to-face with the bellhop, a French boy about her own age. She froze.

"Welcome to Paris," he said with a wink.

"*Merci*," Alexa said in her best French accent, then lingered for a second longer.

Lindsey noticed the way Alexa couldn't stop staring at the Frenchman's chiseled chin and light brown hair. The expression on her daughter's face was probably the same one she'd had when she first met Jack. Lindsey sighed. How could this be happening so soon?

Alexa walked toward her with a smile that wouldn't stop. "I mean, really? Already? We just landed," Lindsey whispered.

As they entered the hotel, Lindsey watched Alexa turn around to find that the bellhop had not taken his eyes off her. Her grin got even bigger. She gave him one last look, then followed Lindsey inside.

The interior of the hotel was even more

charming than the exterior. Ornate wood moldings framed the wallpapered walls. Velvet drapes hung from the windows and gold frames held oil paintings that looked to be well over several hundred years old. Large leather chairs sat across from the front desk, and the small entrance opened into an ivy-laced courtyard in the center of the hotel.

"Bonjour. Bienvenue a' L'hôtel," the desk clerk said.

Alexa opened her mouth to respond, but Lindsey beat her to it. In perfect French, she said, "Thank you, what a beautiful place. We have a reservation for Wilson, please."

"Impressive. And why is your French better than mine?" Alexa asked.

"Because you stopped in twelfth grade?"

Alexa looked perplexed. "Not to worry," the desk clerk said. "Our staff speaks English."

"Good to know," Alexa said.

The clerk searched for the reservation, then turned to Lindsey. "Ah, yes. Your friend Monsieur Hugo had you upgraded to a suite."

"That's so nice," Lindsey said. His thoughtfulness didn't really surprise her. Many times, Hugo had brought her dinner at the studio so that she could paint well into the night with no interruptions.

"Unfortunately, your room won't be ready for a few hours."

"That's okay," Alexa said. "We don't need a room. We're in Paris!"

Lindsey gave a knowing look to the desk clerk. "She's never been here before."

"It's okay. I love when people love my city as much as I do," the clerk said. Alexa shot her mom an I-told-you-so look. "Go. Explore. Enjoy the city. I'll call you when your room's ready. Do you need a map?"

"No. She used to live here," Alexa told the clerk.

"Ah, then you understand your daughter's enthusiasm. No?"

Lindsey smiled. "I guess I do." She recalled her first day in the city, when she'd arrived alone with two suitcases and enough francs to get her to her dorm. Once she'd settled in, she knew she'd be able to access the bank account her parents had set up for her, but until then, she remembered feeling like she was finally on her own. That there was a certain type of magic in the air that would change her life forever.

Today she felt that, too, but the change that was coming scared her. She wasn't ready to have her daughter so far away. She wasn't ready to give up *POV*. What would she do alone in her Brooklyn tower? And what would she do with her life without the magazine?

"Is there somewhere we can get a coffee?"

Alexa asked the desk clerk, then pointed to her mom. "This one didn't sleep much."

"Of course. Go out the door, turn left. Three doors down, there's a little café. Ask for Max and tell him you're a guest of the hotel. He'll give you a discount."

"Thank you," Lindsey said. "We'll see you in a little bit."

Alexa bounded out the door of the hotel with Lindsey in tow. After they got their coffees, they started walking down the street outside the café. Lindsey wrapped her hands around the coffee cup, appreciating its warmth, but the day wasn't really that cold for January. They'd gotten lucky with the mild weather and the bright winter sunshine.

"You know, I have no clue where we are. You have to lead us," Alexa said as she stepped to the side and gestured for Lindsey to walk ahead.

"It would be my pleasure. Where do you want to go?"

"I don't know. Maybe the Arc de Triomphe? I mean, I know we passed it on the ride in, but I want to see it up close. Or the Place de la Concorde." Alexa paused, then pulled out her notebook with the to-see list.

"What about the Louvre?" Lindsey asked. The museum was still one of her favorite places in the entire city.

42

"I don't know. Do we want to save the Louvre till our last day together?"

Lindsey stopped in her tracks, wilting inside. "Can we not use the phrase, 'last day together?'"

It must have shown on the outside, too, because Alexa said, "You're not allowed to get sad yet. We have almost a week."

"It's only four days," Lindsey said matter-of-factly.

"A lot can happen in four days," Alexa said as they crossed the street to have a perfect view of the Seine. The tableau in front of them was similar to the one depicted in the painting that had hung in their place all those years. Both mother and daughter took it all in.

"I know what we should do. We should go to that 'love locks' bridge. Do you know where it is?" Alexa asked.

Lindsey stiffened and turned to her. *Does she know something?*

Alexa frowned. "Don't give me that look, like I just asked you to visit someone in prison. I asked to visit a place of love. Doesn't it sound romantic?"

"It's a bridge. With locks," Lindsey said. The image of her and Jack staring over the railing as their lock fell to the bottom of the river flashed through her mind. A heavy feeling pressed on her chest. "There's nothing special about it."

"But those locks are symbols of people pledging their love to each other," Alexa said wistfully.

Lindsey couldn't deny that fact, but she couldn't face the bridge. At least not today, and certainly not before three more cups of coffee... or maybe two glasses of wine. Even then, she'd probably prefer to go anywhere else. "That's true, but..."

"But what?"

"How many of those people are still together today?" Lindsey asked.

"All of them. In some way," Alexa said.

Lindsey smiled at her daughter's hopeful thought. When Lindsey and Dane had divorced, she'd done her best to shield Alexa from the truth about their love—that it had one day fizzled up and died. For Alexa, love was still special. "I probably said that very thing once," Lindsey said.

"Well, everyone's supposed to fall in love in Paris, aren't they?" Alexa asked.

"Yeah, until they go back to their real lives."

"Wait." Alexa gave her a keen look. "Did you ever fall in love here?"

Lindsey paused. She'd revealed too much.

Should she go ahead and tell Alexa about

Jack? No. There was no real reason for her to explain their relationship. It was so far in the past that it no longer mattered.

"You know what we should do? We should surprise Hugo," Lindsey said, quickly changing the subject.

"Okay, but I know what you did there. You changed the subject. I sense a story."

"There's no story. I was young. I lived in Paris. I painted. I came home. Not too long after that, I had you."

"Sure, Mom. I believe you. So, which way is Hugo's?" Alexa asked.

"East. We need to head east." Lindsey pointed over Alexa's shoulder.

"Great," Alexa did an about-face and followed Lindsey toward the studio.

Hugo's studio was housed in a large Renaissance building with a beige cement façade, blessed with large windows. Inside, Alexa and Lindsey boarded an old elevator, the kind with a metal sliding gate that had to be closed manually. Alexa closed it for them. "Remember when I was a kid and I wanted to be an elevator man who took people to the correct floors?"

"You did love pushing buttons."

"Was that supposed to mean something

else?" Alexa asked, sounding slightly offended.

Oh, dear. That had come out wrong. "Oh my gosh, no. Not at all. You literally loved to push buttons. When you were three, we went to Macy's, and you pushed the button for every single floor. People were so mad." The memory lightened her mood. "But you were so cute. We rode that thing for an hour."

"I *was* cute, wasn't I?"

Lindsey leaned over and gave Alexa a playful kiss on the forehead as the elevator came to a stop. "You still are. Now let's go meet Hugo."

Lindsey knocked on the door and heard a voice call out from inside, "*C'est ouvert!*"

Alexa looked to her mom and whispered, "He said it's open. See, my French isn't terrible."

Lindsey opened the door and Alexa followed her into Hugo's studio, an industrial-looking space with high ceilings, flooded with sunshine from the skylights. There were canvases everywhere, some on easels, some leaning against the walls. The wood floor was covered in spattered paint. It was the place of real artists. Alexa's mouth hung open.

Hugo stood at an easel with his back to them. "*Bonjour*, Ricardo. Put the paints down, and don't make a mess this time!"

Lindsey chuckled. "Charming as ever."

Hugo whirled around, his mouth open with surprise.

He looked much the same as Lindsey remembered him. He still had a full head of hair and a slight moustache and beard, although they were completely white now. As he rushed to greet them, he moved with the lightness of a much younger man. Apparently, the life of an artist continued to agree with him. "My dear Lindsey! And Alexa—my new protégé." He opened his arms and embraced them both.

"Protégé? Well, now I can only disappoint you," Alexa said as they pulled apart.

Hugo took Alexa by the shoulders like a father would and said, "You'll only disappoint me if you stop painting, like your mother did."

"I took some time off, that's all," Lindsey protested.

"Twenty years?" Hugo shook his head.

"I painted my apartment. Navajo white with ecru trim." Okay, that didn't exactly count as artwork, but she was proud of the fact that she didn't have to hire someone to paint her place like everyone else in New York.

Hugo shook his head again. "White, ecru? Have I taught you nothing?"

"It's very livable. And neutral." Lindsey

liked the way her home looked. It was inviting and sophisticated all at once.

"Neutral? That's the color of canvas before you paint it," Hugo pointed out.

"I couldn't agree more," Alexa said. "Why use neutrals when you have a whole palette of color?"

Hugo patted Alexa on the back. "A genius already. This is going to be fun working together."

"Thank you so much for recommending me to the program," Alexa said. "It's so great to finally meet you in person."

"I promise you will love the university. And your favorite class will be mine." Lindsey and Alexa laughed with him. "And until you move into the dorms, I hope you like my hotel recommendation."

"We love it," Lindsey said as Alexa nodded her head in agreement. "And thank you for the upgrade. Who did you bribe?"

Hugo flashed a smile that made his silver beard twitch. "Turns out I know the manager."

Lindsey laughed again. "Same old Hugo. Friends with half of Paris."

"How else am I going to sell my art?" he exclaimed as he pointed to the various canvases around the room.

Well, he had a point there. Lindsey walked over to one of the landscapes and inspected it more closely. The brushstrokes, the sense of color... "Is it possible you've gotten even better?"

"Of course it is. I'm like a fine wine," Hugo said. He walked them around the studio, showing them some of his favorite recent works. As they rounded a corner, Hugo stopped and pointed to an unfinished painting. It was a landscape of the Pont des Arts bridge with love locks affixed to the rail.

"What do you think of this one?" Hugo asked Alexa.

"The love locks!" she exclaimed. "It's beautiful. Why isn't it finished?"

"Ask your mother," Hugo said.

Alexa looked to her mom, her eyes wide. "That's yours? So, you *do* know where the locks are."

Lindsey nodded as she scanned her old painting. It had been a long time since she'd seen it last, yet it remained familiar. The orange sky was better than she'd remembered, but it still wasn't that perfect blood orange she'd seen on that long-ago afternoon at the top of the Eiffel Tower.

"I can't believe you kept that," Lindsey said as she turned to Hugo.

"Why wouldn't I? It might be your best work. If you ever finished it."

No way. She couldn't finish it back then, so how would she finish it now? It was missing that element she'd lost her chance at, years ago: the presence and the experience of someone who had sealed her lock on the bridge.

"Some things are better off left unfinished," she said. When she'd returned to New York, she'd left the painting behind on purpose. She didn't want the memory, yet she couldn't bear to destroy her own work. She'd hid it in the back of Hugo's studio, hoping that he'd find it years after she was gone and forget it was hers. Like most painters she'd known, he often re-used canvases to save money. She'd thought that maybe he'd do that with her painting, using it to create something beautiful and new, and she'd never have to see it again. But now, here it was—staring her in the face, reminding her of her time with Jack.

"Maybe you'll change your mind while you're here," Hugo said, interrupting her train of thought. "And finish it."

"I wouldn't count on that." She had no intention of picking up a paintbrush while she was in Paris. She was strictly there to ensure her daughter felt settled and ready for the semester, and she had no interest in a trip down memory lane.

"We'll see," Hugo said with a smile.

"No. Really. I'm not painting." Lindsey

placed a hand on her daughter's shoulder. "Alexa's here to paint."

"Fine. Well, at least you'll be here for my show," Hugo said.

"I wouldn't miss it," Lindsey said.

A few minutes later, her phone buzzed with a message from the hotel. "Our suite's ready," she told Alexa, then turned to Hugo. "We'll see you soon?"

"Of course. Stop by anytime. And seriously, this canvas is yours to finish if you want. You can use all of my supplies."

Lindsey shook her head. "Thanks, Hugo, but I've moved on." As she and Alexa left, she felt grateful that Hugo hadn't brought up the story of Jack and the love locks bridge.

"Hugo's nice, isn't he?" Lindsey asked her as they left the studio.

"Are you kidding? He's more than nice. He's inspiring. I can't wait to start painting."

"And I can't wait to see what you paint." Lindsey would enjoy seeing scenes of Paris through the eyes of her daughter, who had yet to be jaded by love and life.

Chapter Four

Traveling Back

IT WAS JUST AFTER THREE o'clock when Alexa and her mother made it back to the hotel. The desk clerk had given them their keys and escorted them to their top-floor suite. The suite was complete with a living room and two bedrooms, each with its own bathroom. Alexa had seen suites in movies, but this was something else. She felt like they were staying in a castle. The four-poster beds, the satin comforters, and big down decorative pillows all made it feel like she was a little girl entering a big girl's world.

"I'm never going to be able to go to the dorms after this," Alexa said as she walked through the first bedroom. Her dorm in Connecticut was half the size of this bedroom. The walls were cinder blocks painted with shiny paint so they wouldn't stain, and her long, narrow twin bed was nowhere near as luxurious as the one she was about to sleep on, no matter how high the thread count of her sheets were. After seeing this suite, Alexa was pretty sure her dorm in Paris would be far better than anything she could find back in the States.

Lindsey followed Alexa into the second bedroom. "I'm never going to be able to go back to anything," Lindsey said.

Alexa flopped onto her bed. "I think I'm already in love."

"Me too. And exhausted," Lindsey replied. "I'm going to take a shower and a nap. Will you be okay by yourself?"

Alexa looked out the window at the bustling street below and the Seine in the distance. "With this view? I think I can manage."

"Well, don't go wandering around here. It's almost dark. Stay in your room?"

"Mom, you're helicoptering again."

Her mother looked guilty. "I know."

"Don't worry. I have no clue where I'm going anyway. I'll be right here when you wake up," Alexa said as she ushered her mom to the door.

"We'll do dinner then," Lindsey said, then did the European double kiss and walked into her room. "Good night."

"Sweet dreams," Alexa replied as she closed the door.

Alexa opened her smaller suitcase and started to unpack. She'd brought two specific bags, one for the hotel for the next four days and one that held the rest of her clothes for the next few months. She pulled out her toiletries and brought them into the bathroom. The counters were marble and the brass faucets gleamed like gold. There was even a claw-foot bathtub and a big plushy robe hanging behind the door. This was far better than the shared bathrooms she'd had to get used to at school on the East Coast. Alexa decided she'd take a bath, then unpack the rest of her clothes. She might as well enjoy the life of luxury while she could.

After her bath, Alexa wrapped herself in the super soft robe and unpacked her clothes, hanging each item in the armoire next to the bed. When she finished, she got into bed and grabbed her phone. She was about to log in to the WiFi network and check in on social media when she caught a glimpse outside. The winter sun was beginning to set, and the sky was turning pink.

She put her phone on the nightstand and threw the drapes wide open so that she'd have a better view. She became transfixed on the scene outside. *Paris is magic.* Anywhere else, she'd be snapping photos and uploading them instantly for her followers to see, but here, she had no desire to share—she simply wanted to be in the moment. To absorb the colors and the emotions. The smell of history and her freshly scrubbed skin now coated with a French lotion she knew hadn't come from the local drugstore. In Connecticut, and even New York, she'd never been so inspired. She'd been painting for years, but she'd never had this kind of feeling—where the present moment was all that mattered. She'd always been living in the past or the future, thinking of what had been and what would be, painting what she thought others wanted to see.

She took a deep breath as the sky turned a deeper shade of pink with a hint of orange. The sun drifted lower on the horizon.

Just as it was about to disappear for the night, she picked up her phone and snapped a quick photo. She couldn't resist. Though the moment was etched into her mind, she knew she would use the color in a painting one day, and she'd had enough schooling to know that a color is hard to match if you don't have a photo.

As Alexa was about to turn away from the window, she looked down into the street and caught a glimpse of the bellhop from earlier that day. She was staring at him when he looked up. Alexa froze. Could he see her? She yanked at her robe, although it was closed tight.

He smiled and waved. Feeling both flirtatious and shy, Alexa turned left and right as if she was looking to see if he was gesturing to someone else. He shook his head and pointed right at her. Then he smiled and waved again. Slowly, she lifted her right hand away from her robe and responded with a tiny flicker of her fingers. Then he made a gesture to say, *Come down here.*

Her stomach fluttered. Should she go down and meet him? She shrugged her shoulders as if she didn't understand. He made the come-hither gesture again.

Oh, why not? She held up her hand, fingers spread wide to indicate she needed five minutes. He smiled and pointed inside the hotel.

Alexa closed the drapes and threw off her robe. *What should I wear?* She didn't want to look as if she was trying too hard, but appearing like a complete slob was not an option either. She opened the armoire and looked at her clothes. Nothing appealed to her. Then she remembered her gray cashmere sweater that she had packed in the bigger suitcase for when she arrived at school. She tore it open and dug through the stacks of clothes until she found it.

She put it on, pulled on a pair of jeans, and looked in the mirror. The sweater was conservative but fitted enough to show off her figure. She put on her boots, then applied a fresh coat of lip gloss. She smacked her lips together to even out the color and made a popping sound. *This is Paris,* she thought. *Living on a whim, in the moment.* Alexa grabbed her jacket and quickly headed out. Just as the door clicked shut behind her, she realized she had not only left the key behind, but also her phone. She was locked out.

She contemplated knocking on the door and waking up her mom, but didn't want to have to deal with a barrage of questions. *Where are you going? Who are you meeting? What are you doing?* Plus, her mom had looked really tired earlier. If she was still asleep, Alexa didn't want to wake her. She decided to leave her phone behind and head downstairs. Best-case scenario, she'd be back before her mom even noticed. Worst-case scenario, her mom would wake up and come looking for her. Either way, she'd still be in the hotel, and there was no way her mom could get mad at her for that. She'd simply tell her that she got hungry.

When the elevator reached the ground floor, Alexa exited to find the bellhop waiting in the courtyard. His back was toward her, but she knew it was him. She straightened out her jacket, fluffed up her hair, and started walking his way. Just as she was about to tap on his shoulder, he turned around. Alexa jumped.

"*Mademoiselle,* I'm so sorry," he said. "I didn't mean to scare you."

"It's okay." A tiny tingle went through her body. His eyes were mesmerizing.

"I'm Jean Paul, but everyone calls me J.P.," he said as he reached out for a proper handshake greeting.

"I'm Alexa," she said as she put her hand in his. He leaned in closer, and Alexa paused for a moment. *Is he going to kiss me already?*

"It's very nice to meet you," he said. "We never got to properly meet earlier today."

"No, we didn't," Alexa said as she thought back to the first time she caught his eye—and the second time. "So, do you always look up to the suite?"

"Not at all. I guess today I just got lucky. Also, I might have overheard the desk clerk say you'd been upgraded," J.P. said with a smile.

"Oh, so you're a stalker," Alexa teased. "I thought French men were smoother than that."

"I thought American women were more cautious than to meet up with strangers."

"*Touché.* We are. I just happened to want to come downstairs for a latte," Alexa said lightly.

"Oh, I see. Then I shall get you a latte. Should we sit over there?" J.P. pointed to a little table in the middle of the courtyard under the twinkling lights. Alexa nodded. "You go sit and I'll get us the drinks."

"Thank you," Alexa said as she watched J.P. walk off. Seeing him in his street clothes made him even more attractive. While she liked the bellhop uniform, he now looked more casual and fun, like the kind of guy she could see herself spending more time with.

A few minutes later, J.P. returned with their lattes and took a seat across from Alexa.

"So, where are you from?" he asked.

"New York. But I go to school in Connecticut."

"I've always wanted to visit New York," J.P. said, and took a sip of his latte.

"And I've always wanted to come here," she replied. Paris had been on her mind since she was a young girl, and she thought she knew exactly what it would be like when she arrived, yet everything was already different and completely exceeding her expectations.

"How long are you staying?"

"For a semester. At the Sorbonne," she said.

J.P.'s face lit up. "Really? I'm there, too. Third year."

Alexa couldn't help but smile. What were the chances that the first day she was in Paris she would meet someone from her school? "What are you studying?"

"Mathematics. You?"

"Art."

"I love art," J.P. said.

"I love math," Alexa blurted out before she could even think about what she was saying.

"Really?"

She could feel herself blushing. "I could. I mean, everyone needs to know math, right?"

J.P. laughed. "Of course they do," he said reassuringly, then placed his hand on top of hers.

Alexa took a deep breath.

"Tell me about art. Do you draw, sculpt, paint?" he asked.

Thank goodness, he was smoothing over her awkwardness. "I paint," she said. "My mom paints, too. Well, she used to. She studied here when she was in college."

"Is that why you paint?"

Alexa thought for a moment. No one had ever asked her that question. "I guess, in a way, yes. When I was growing up, there was this painting of Paris that my mom had done that hung in our hallway for years. I always thought the image of Paris and the feelings it gave me made me want to paint. But I guess it was really my mom. She used to tell me story upon story about her mentor, an artist named Hugo, and I always felt he was like an uncle I'd never gotten to meet."

"Are you going to meet him while you're here?"

"I already did. He's every bit what I imagined," Alexa said, remembering how expansive Hugo's studio was and how welcoming he had been.

"That's amazing," J.P. said.

"I'm going to study with him while I'm here." Alexa took another sip of her latte. "Tell me about you. I've been blabbing too much."

"What do you want to know?"

"I don't know. How did you choose math?" Alexa asked. She'd always thought of it as boring… however, J.P. seemed anything but.

"My father is an economist, and we always talked numbers at the dinner table. Also, I don't have one creative bone in my body. Math was easy for me."

"I was the opposite," Alexa said. "I'm creative but terrible at math."

"I guess that's a good thing," J.P. said with a smile. "What do they say? Opposites attract?"

Alexa nodded. "Yes, they do."

There was a moment of silence between them. Then J.P. said, "I don't know if this is too forward, but I have the day off tomorrow. Maybe I could show you around."

Alexa's heartbeat sped up a little at the invitation. "I'd love that. But I'll be with my mom. She's going through this empty-nest thing."

"Empty nest. You mean, like a bird?" He looked utterly confused.

"More like a raptor guarding an egg." If Alexa wasn't eighteen, she'd definitely be getting grounded tonight for leaving the room.

"I'm not sure I understand." He traced the top of his mug with his pointer finger.

"Me either. But I love her." Despite her mom being a little overbearing, she loved that they had a close relationship. So many of her friends could barely stand their mothers and couldn't wait to get to college. Alexa, on the other hand, missed her mom when she was away at school. Granted, it wasn't the kind of missing your mom that happens in third grade when you go off to summer camp and only want to go home, but she missed their banter and their late-night chats while she was away.

When Lindsey awoke from her much-needed nap, she was shocked to see that it was already dark. "Alexa?" she called out, half-expecting her daughter to bound in and jump on her bed like she had as a kid.

But Alexa didn't come running and there was no response. Lindsey got out of bed and trudged over to Alexa's room only to find it empty. She went back to her own part of the suite and picked up her phone to call Alexa and see where she was. It was later than she'd expected. Alexa had probably gotten hungry and gone downstairs for some food.

She dialed Alexa, but two seconds later, she heard the phone ring in the other room. Now Lindsey was worried. She quickly got dressed. With any luck, the desk clerk would've seen which way she went.

Lindsey rode the elevator down and stepped out into the lobby. She looked around, but there was no Alexa to be found, only a bunch of couples sitting together on a few of the sofas near the fireplace.

Sitting on a red leather sofa and reading a book was a woman with light brown hair who looked to be in her sixties. Lindsey approached. "Excuse me, I seem to have lost my daughter. Have you seen her?"

The woman turned around, concerned. "Oh dear. How old is the child?" She had a British accent.

Lindsey felt sheepish. "Actually, eighteen."

The woman smiled knowingly. "Not lost then. Just being eighteen."

Lindsey felt a sudden sense of connection with this woman. "That's what I'm afraid of. We just got here. I took a nap. And she left."

"I'm sure she's fine. I did see a young woman in the courtyard with Jean Paul."

Lindsey flashed back to their arrival that morning. "Jean Paul. Is he a bellhop?"

The woman nodded. "Yes, I think he does a little of everything around here. A lovely young man."

"Thank you," Lindsey said as she headed off to the courtyard.

She trudged outside and found Alexa and the bellhop sitting alone in the cold, laughing. "Alexa, there you are."

Alexa turned around, a look of embarrassment on her face. The young man quickly stood up to greet her.

"Mom, this is Jean Paul."

"Madame. You needn't worry about your nest," he said enthusiastically, perhaps trying to impress her.

"What?" Lindsey asked.

He looked flustered. "Uh... enjoy your evening," he said as he walked back to the lobby.

"You scared him away," Alexa complained. Maybe she hadn't had a chance to make plans to see him again.

"If he scares that easily, he's not for you," Lindsey advised.

"And you know that how?"

The words cut her. Of course, it wasn't as if Lindsey had ever really dated after the divorce. Alexa probably figured she didn't know anything about love or men who scared easily. Still, Lindsey knew her daughter wasn't trying to hurt her feelings, so she kept her voice even. "Because, sweetie, he lives in Paris. Chances are, whatever you start now is going to end in three months."

"End? It hasn't even begun." Alexa pouted.

Lindsey was giving solid advice, even if she sounded a little brash. "I know you think I'm just your mother, but I was you once. What happens if you fall in love with this Jean Paul?"

"I just met him. I'm not falling in love." Impatience edged her voice, and Lindsey couldn't really blame her. Alexa had met plenty of boys before in New York, and Lindsey never cautioned her this much. She didn't know why she was overdoing it now, but she couldn't seem to help herself.

"Exactly. You're not falling in love now. But what about when the semester's over and you're going home, and you realize you'll probably never see him again? That will ruin Paris for you. And all the excitement you feel right now being here will be ruined, too. Because you'll just be reminded of him." After Lindsey let out the final word, she realized she'd gone too far.

Alexa looked at her mom with a perplexed look.

"Look, I don't know what's going on with

you. Maybe it's jet lag, but I'm going up to the room to change," Alexa said. She then took her mom by the shoulders and led her back into the lobby. "And you're going to the bar, where you're going to get a nice glass of wine and remind yourself that I'm an adult."

Lindsey sighed. She had definitely gone too far with her words of wisdom. "Okay, you're right. I will have a glass of wine while you change, and then we'll go to dinner."

"Now you sound more like my mother," Alexa said as she squeezed her mom's shoulders. "Let me have the key, please." She smiled, then headed to the elevator.

Lindsey walked up to the small hotel bar. There was no sense denying it to herself: seeing Alexa with Jean Paul had brought back too many memories of Jack. Their relationship ended twenty years ago, and Lindsey now ran a successful business, one that someone wanted to buy. She'd gotten over Jack a long time ago. Yet, somehow, he was back on her mind. She'd always thought he'd ruined her recollections of Paris when she was young, and she couldn't let him ruin her time here now. This trip was supposed to be about Alexa, about their mother-daughter time.

"Pardon," Lindsey said to the bartender who was mixing drinks with his back to her. "I'll have a glass of white wine, please."

"Sure, we have a very nice..." the bartender began as he turned around with a bottle of wine in his hand.

Lindsey's mouth dropped at the sight of the man. "Oh my..."

It couldn't be.

But it was. Jack. Twenty years older, with shorter hair, but just as handsome.

"Lindsey?" Jack's eyes widened. He appeared to be as shocked to see her as she was to see him.

"Jack?" She had to ask the question again as if somehow that might make it less real. "What are you doing here?"

"Looks like I'm pouring you a drink."

Jack had thought about this moment for years. He'd even scripted the perfect speech for when he saw her again. It was supposed to be an apology for not making it to New York when they'd planned... and yet, now that it was actually happening, he could barely muster a few words.

"You're the bartender?" she asked. No doubt she was thinking that at least she hadn't missed out on much.

"Actually, I kind of own the place."

She looked even more astonished, if that was possible. And why wouldn't she be? After he'd failed to show up in New York City, she'd probably given up on the idea of him becoming an adult. In her head, he'd probably always been the immature guy who couldn't commit.

"I think I'm going to need the bottle," she said as he uncorked the wine.

"You and me both," Jack said as he poured her a giant glass of wine. "I guess if there's ever a time to overserve, it's now."

Jack dumped some wine into a glass for himself as Lindsey smiled and swallowed a big gulp.

Jack took a giant sip and the two stared at each other in silence. He didn't know what to say next, and apparently, neither did she.

Chapter Five

A Reflection

LINDSEY NERVOUSLY SPUN HER GLASS around by the stem. She was in shock. Although being in Paris had brought back a flood of memories already, seeing Jack in person was a whole other deal. She didn't know what to do or say. When she was younger, she'd imagined how the scene would play out if they ever saw each other again. She'd scold him and make him feel terrible for never coming to New York, then she'd go on to tell him that he was too late, she'd already met someone else. He'd had his chance and he'd lost it. She was with Dane now. They were married and in love. They had a baby...

But that scene was supposed to happen when she was twenty-five. She was forty now, and the whole thing seemed petty, not to mention that she was no longer with Dane—she was actually single. Now, if he apologized, she wouldn't be able to tell him off. She might have to accept the apology.

Lindsey took a sip of her wine.

"Do you like it?" Jack asked. "We got it in from Italy last week. It's a new blend of some of their older grapes."

"It's nice." Lindsey placed her nose inside the rim to inhale the full bouquet. "Very fruit forward." She pretended to be an ordinary customer, just as Jack was treating her.

"I see your palette's gotten a little more sophisticated since our twenties," Jack said.

"I should hope so." Lindsey smiled.

Jack held up his glass and took a deep breath of the flavor. "A hint of citrus with a little peach." He took a sip and swirled it around his tongue. "Not bad," he said.

Lindsey took another sip and nodded. This was so absurd. So much history between them, and they were talking about wine. There was a long moment of silence between them.

Finally, Jack interrupted it. "I still can't believe you're here."

"Well, Hugo didn't tell me this was your hotel," Lindsey explained with a sigh.

"I was wondering why he called me out of the blue. I didn't recognize your last name." Jack took a bigger sip of wine.

"It's my married name," Lindsey replied. Jack's face dropped. Lindsey felt a surge of satisfaction, but made an effort to hide it. It wasn't the same as being able to tell him that he'd missed his chance, but it was something to watch him wince at the thought of her being married.

"Congratulations," he said.

"We're divorced," Lindsey stated. Jack's face lit up. *At least the victory lasted for a few seconds.*

"My condolences," Jack said.

"Thank you and thank you," Lindsey said. It was strange that she had literally explained the past twenty years of her love life in two sentences. This was certainly not the meeting with Jack she'd pictured in her mind forever ago. It was supposed to be far more dramatic than married and divorced.

"So, are you here to see Hugo? Obviously, it wasn't to see me," Jack said with a curl of his lips. "What are you doing here?"

"I'm dropping off my daughter at school," Lindsey said. At least that was one great part of her life she could brag about.

"You have a daughter," Jack said.

"Her name's Alexa. She's studying art." Lindsey wanted to tell him all the details. How her daughter was talented and one of her best friends. How they had a special bond and how she was incredibly worried that Alexa would fall in love in Paris and get her heart broken just as she had.

"Like mother, like daughter." Jack took another sip of wine.

"Art imitates life, I guess. You have kids?" Lindsey asked. Even though she couldn't picture Jack with kids, it was a fair question. She had to assume he had dated women over the years and possibly even married.

"No. Just a hotel," Jack replied.

"Well, your hotel is a great place." As Lindsey brought her glass of wine to her lips again, she looked around at the impeccable decorating and the art on the walls.

"I took it over a while ago," Jack said. "It's going on ten years now."

It shouldn't have surprised Lindsey that Jack had grown up, but it did. In her head, he was still the twenty-year-old jerk who'd never shown up for her. Now Lindsey was seeing a different side of him. A responsible side.

She took another sip of wine. "You cut your hair," she said.

Jack ran his fingers through his brown locks. "Yeah, that's going on twenty years," he said. She wondered if his dad had forced him to cut it. His father had never liked longer hair. He was of the opinion that longer hair was unprofessional. Jack used to complain all the time about the way his father nagged him. *"If you want to make it in this* business," he'd said, "you got to play the part. No distractions."

Lindsey had always encouraged Jack to do his own thing, but back then, he was young enough to believe his father and follow his instructions. Father knows best, he'd always said, and done as he was told. Jack took another sip of wine and looked straight into Lindsey's eyes.

"You look..." he started.

"Older?" Lindsey cut in.

"I was going to say beautiful," he said.

Lindsey blushed and spun the stem of her wineglass around again and again. "Thank you," she managed to mutter, completely flustered.

For a moment, they said nothing as they looked into each other's eyes. It was as if time had never passed and they were twenty years old again, yet everything was different. Lindsey didn't know what to say next. Should she talk about the past? Or focus on the present? Lindsey looked to him for a clue, but he seemed distracted.

"You look just like your mom," Jack said as he looked past Lindsey.

Lindsey turned around and saw Alexa. She approached.

"Hi, Mom. Good, you got that glass of wine and a nice bartender to help you," Alexa said.

"Yes. I did." Oh, this was awkward. "Alexa, this is Jack. He's..." What should she call him?

"An old friend," he said. Alexa grinned. Lindsey tried to cover by flashing a bigger grin, but she knew Alexa could see right through her.

"Nice to meet you," Alexa said then turned to her mom. "Funny, you never mentioned him."

"I'm sure I did," Lindsey stated in an effort to let Jack know that she hadn't forgotten about him—or forgiven him—even if she was lying.

"No. You didn't," Alexa said.

"It was a long time ago," Lindsey said. No matter how old kids got, they had a way of telling the truth at the most inopportune times. When Alexa was five, she liked to tell anyone who would listen at the grocery store that her mom was lactose intolerant and milk gave her gas.

"It seems like just yesterday that we knew each other." Jack smiled. Lindsey felt more uncomfortable by the moment. She realized she was pushing her lips together the way she used to do when she was nervous to show a new painting. Did Jack notice how anxious she was?

She just needed to get out of there quickly. "It's late. We should get going."

"Actually, it's eight," Alexa replied.

"It's late in New York."

"I'm pretty sure it's earlier in New York," Jack said.

But Lindsey didn't want to hear it. She finished off her glass of wine and pushed her stool away from the bar. "It was nice seeing you," she said as she gathered up her coat.

"Chances are you'll be seeing a lot of me. You need some extra towels, I'm your guy," Jack said. Lindsey pushed her lips together once more, then walked away with Alexa in tow.

Why hadn't Hugo given her the heads-up that Jack owned the hotel? She couldn't believe it.

Outside, Lindsey walked quickly toward the river, Alexa tried to keep pace. "Whoa, speedy. You want to slow down a bit?"

Lindsey kept powering forward. "We need to change hotels." Her mind was spinning.

Alexa took a few quick steps and caught up with her. "But I like this hotel. I don't want to move."

"You'll adjust," Lindsey said with that mom tone of *you'll have to make do with what you're given.*

"We're not moving," Alexa insisted. "I just unpacked."

Lindsey didn't want to hear Alexa's laments and continued walking. She took a deep breath. There was something about the air that came off the Seine that had always helped her clear her mind.

"So, who is he?" Alexa asked.

Ugh. What should she say? Sugarcoat it, or tell the truth? "Just someone I knew from the Sorbonne," she said. "He was finishing his degree. His father was in the hotel business here."

"And?" Alexa asked.

"And I went home to finish college. He was supposed to follow me, but he didn't." Lindsey hadn't exactly lied. That was the truth of what happened, yet it wasn't the full story.

"And that's it?" Alexa asked, obviously unsatisfied with Lindsey's answer.

"We called, we wrote. Time passed. And life happened. I met your dad. You know the rest." Saying it out loud made it seem a little less harsh, because meeting Dane had given her Alexa, and that was all worth it.

"You were in love," Alexa said. Lindsey shrugged. "Mom, this is fate."

The way Alexa's face lit up at the word *fate* made Lindsey's stomach flip.

"This is not fate. This is Hugo meddling. Just like the old days."

"Did Hugo introduce you two?" Alexa pried.

Lindsey shook her head no. "He didn't

introduce us, but he did love us together. He used to say we were made for each other."

"Maybe you still are." Alexa smiled.

"I doubt it. Too much time has passed." Lindsey didn't even want to think about re-kindling everything with Jack. It was too confusing and messy... and it would only lead to new heartbreak. She was here to bring Alexa to school then return to New York and figure out what to do with the magazine.

"You never know," Alexa said as they stepped onto the nearest bridge. Lindsey took a deep breath of the fresh air. "Maybe you'll get back together."

"I doubt it," Lindsey said and kept walking out onto the bridge.

"Wait. Why not? Look at where we are." Alexa pointed to the railing of the bridge. "We found it. It's the love locks bridge. I would take this as a sign if I were you."

"It's definitely not a sign," Lindsey said and took another deep breath of air.

They were on the Pont Neuf bridge. Lindsey looked around. It wasn't the Pont des Arts bridge where she and Jack had once attempted to seal their love with a lock, but it was eerily similar, and covered in thousands of locks. The romance had spread to the other bridges over the Seine. She was astounded. "There's so many now," she pondered aloud.

Alexa ran her hand along the locks. "Look at all that love. It's beautiful," she said.

"They're all rusted." What would've happened to hers and Jack's, if it had made it onto the bridge, instead of falling to the bottom of the river?

"The rust just means they lasted," Alexa said. Lindsey had to smile. There was something refreshing about the young's perspective of love. It was the kind of vision that you can only have before your heart's been broken too many times.

Lindsey ran her hands along the locks. She'd had that vision once, too.

"Maybe it's time to finish that painting of yours Hugo hung on to," Alexa said.

Lindsey shook her head as she took in her surroundings. The scene was far different from what she remembered. She didn't know if it was the amount of locks, or the rust, or the fact that she was now looking at a different bridge through eyes that had seen too much heartache, but she didn't feel the same way about the locks as she once did. There was no way she could finish the painting now. It would never look right. "I don't think I'll be finishing that painting," she told Alexa. "But I think it's time for you to paint a new one." Lindsey didn't want to talk about Jack or the love locks anymore.

"Okay," Alexa said. "Do you want to go? I'm starving."

"Absolutely," Lindsey said. "I know a great little place a few blocks from here."

"Perfect."

Lindsey ushered Alexa off the bridge as quickly as she could.

Seeing Jack was enough for one night. She didn't need to go into all the details about the painting, their lock, and the fact that he'd broken her heart. All Alexa needed to know was that she and Jack had dated once—that was it.

After dinner, Alexa and Lindsey made their way back to the hotel. Luckily, Jack had left for the night, and Lindsey was able to go to bed without another mention of him.

However, that didn't mean he was out of her mind.

Chapter Six

Sunbreak to Heartache

WHEN THE SUN ROSE OVER Paris, Lindsey stirred in her bed. A faint glow of yellow peeked through the curtains. She pulled the covers over her head and turned away from the window. It was far too early to be awake. Running into Jack last night had made sleep difficult, and she needed to rest for a little while longer.

After she and Alexa had come back to the hotel and parted ways for bed, Lindsey had lain in hers for nearly three hours before her eyes would close. She couldn't stop thinking about him. She'd tried to get him out of her head ever since the year he was supposed to meet her on the top of the Empire State Building, and for the most part, she'd succeeded. Now, he permeated her entire consciousness.

Why did he have to look so good?

She'd recounted all the moments she

and Jack had spent together. There were more good memories than bad. She remembered their bike rides and how he'd always taken the time to lock her bike up for her. It was the coed equivalent of opening a door for a woman. He'd been a gentleman who made sure she never had to walk home alone when she painted late into the night. He'd made her laugh and had known every one of her quirks. But that was twenty years ago. What did he know about the woman she was now? Almost nothing.

She'd thought about all the mistakes she'd made in her twenties and wondered if now was the time to forgive Jack. His blue eyes still sparkled the way they used to every afternoon after class when he'd ride with her back to her dorm—but that didn't mean they should rekindle the flame.

She had a grown daughter now and a business that was her sole focus. She didn't need Jack in her life any more than he probably needed her. By this point, she never thought they'd see each other again.

Before she'd finally fallen asleep, at two in the morning, she'd decided she and Jack could reconnect and catch up, but nothing would come out of this time together. It would be just like meeting up with an old friend, like Hugo.

There would be nothing more than the comfort of familiarity.

When the sun's glow could no longer be ignored, Lindsey opened her eyes and stretched in her bed. Time to face the day.

She turned to grab her phone and check the time and found that Alexa was already wide-awake and dressed. She was sitting in the chair by the armoire and moving her finger across her phone.

"Ahhh, the sound of texting in the morning," Lindsey said. It had been a while since she'd woken to the *clicks* of an iPhone. In the months leading up to Alexa's move to college, Alexa had a habit of curling up in her mom's bed early in the morning with her phone in hand. Most of the texting was to friends or messaging on social media, but Lindsey had gotten used to it, and when Alexa had left for Connecticut, she'd missed it.

"You're awake," Alexa said, barely looking up.

"And you're smiling at your phone, which means it's a boy," Lindsey said as she sat up in bed.

"It's J.P.," Alexa said as she sent another text.

"Yesterday he was 'Jean Paul,'" Lindsey reminded Alexa. Were they getting too close already?

"That was yesterday," Alexa said. She

read one of the texts. "Would it be okay if he took me to the university to register for classes?"

Lindsey winced. "Oh, I thought I was doing that." She'd planned the whole day. They'd register Alexa for classes, stop for croissants at her favorite bakery next to the school, and then decide what landmark to visit together.

"It's just that he's registering, too. And he can show me around." Alexa looked up from her phone. Lindsey's dismay must've shown on her face, because Alexa said, "Actually, I'll tell him no."

Lindsey suddenly felt bad and recalled what she had decided last night. She was going to reconnect with Jack; there was nothing wrong with the fact that they'd once fallen in love. In fact, the memories were sweet. Who was she to hold Alexa back from creating her own memories? "You know what? Tell him yes. You two go explore the school together."

"You sure?"

Lindsey nodded. "It'll be good for you to meet some students."

Alexa came over and gave her a big hug. "Love you, Mom."

"Love you, too."

Alexa headed to the door. "Thanks, Mom. I'll see you later today."

"Where are you going? Don't you want

breakfast?" Lindsey asked. She'd said Alexa and J.P. could register together, but she didn't realize that meant Alexa would be leaving right away.

"J.P.'s waiting downstairs. We're going to eat on the way. Bye, Mom," Alexa said as she bounced out of the room.

The door closed before Lindsey even had a chance to respond.

She sighed, then walked over to the window and opened the drapes to let the sun flood the room. The view of the Seine was especially pretty in the morning, and she watched how the winter wind caused ripples in the water. She was about to turn back to bed when she caught a glimpse of Alexa hopping onto the back of J.P.'s Vespa.

"You didn't say he drove a motorcycle!" Lindsey called through the double-paned glass, though she knew Alexa couldn't hear her.

She watched as Alexa put her arms around J.P.'s waist and they disappeared into traffic. Lindsey shook her head. At least when she was Alexa's age, they only rode bicycles. No one could get in trouble then. What was Alexa riding into?

Lindsey walked to the armoire and gathered her clothes, then headed into the bathroom. She didn't want to sit around all day.

Even if Alexa wasn't with her, she could still explore the city.

Downstairs in the dining room, Lindsey sat at a table alone with a cup of coffee. She had ordered a croissant, a fruit plate, and two eggs over easy, but all that had arrived so far was the croissant. She nibbled at it slowly as the fireplace roared next to her.

She gazed into the fire and was about to take another sip of coffee when Jack approached with his own mug. He set it down and sat across from her. Lindsey didn't say a word, still too distracted by the image of Alexa on the back of J.P.'s scooter. "Don't worry, he's a good driver," Jack said.

"You saw them take off this morning?" Lindsey asked, surprised Jack understood her concern.

Jack nodded.

"He better be better than you were," Lindsey said, remembering the one and only time she and Jack rode a scooter.

"That was one bad turn." Jack smiled.

"It was a one-way street," Lindsey reminded him.

"I was only going one way."

"Yes, and I also remember that that was the last time I rode with you anywhere," Lindsey said.

"We rode together all the time," Jack said.

"On bikes, that was it," Lindsey replied remembering their daily route through Paris.

"It was still fun," Jack replied. Lindsey nodded. He handed Lindsey a copy of *The New York Times*. "I brought you this."

Lindsey looked at it and smiled. "You remembered."

"Of course I remembered. I used to go to my dad's hotel every Sunday afternoon and pick through the guests' unread papers and find the crossword for you. I know it's not Sunday, but I thought you could still do the puzzle." Jack took a sip of his café au lait.

"You are quite the host," Lindsey said in disbelief that he'd remembered how she used to love the puzzles.

"Yep, I do it all." Jack leaned forward, as though getting down to business. "So what are you painting these days?"

Lindsey didn't know how to respond. She was immersed in the art world, but it had been years since she'd picked up a paintbrush. "My nails?"

He looked at her with a blank face. "Seriously?"

"I don't really paint anymore."

Jack's expression went slack with shock. "You're kidding. Why?" His reaction didn't surprise her at all. Art had been her life when she was with Jack. It was the reason she couldn't stay in Paris.

"I run an art magazine. It's just in New York, but it's got a following," Lindsey said. Though she was proud of what she'd accomplished, she knew Jack understood how much painting had meant to her. Maybe there would be a small part of him that would wonder if she'd given up too soon. Perhaps there was a small part of herself that wondered the same thing.

"That's great, Lindsey. I can't believe you have a whole magazine."

His praise dispelled her doubts. "Thanks. It's not what I planned, but it's turned out well."

"Life is what happens when you're making plans. I guess we both know that," Jack said. They shared a small smile. It was a truth she knew all too well.

"How's your father?" Lindsey asked, breaking up the moment.

"He took over a hotel in Nice," Jack said. "Once I got started here, he kind of left me alone."

"That sounds nice, or should I say 'Nice?'" Lindsey said with a terrible French accent.

"I'm sorry about, back then..." Jack started.

Oh God. Here it comes. The apology.

"My dad convinced me I needed to stay

on and help with the business. And after a while, so much time had passed…"

Lindsey shook her head. She didn't need to hear any more. It would only make her upset, and what would be the point of that? She knew Jack's dad had never been her biggest fan. He thought artists were likely to wind up homeless, and that a smart woman in her position should've focused on something else. "It's okay. Really. You don't need to go on."

"Okay," Jack said.

Lindsey could sense he wanted to say more, but she couldn't quite deal with the apology. She preferred to sweep it under the rug and forget it.

"I don't know what we were thinking, anyway," Lindsey said. "We had our whole lives in front of us, and we were going to decide them then and there."

"We weren't thinking. We were in love," Jack said.

His words made her feel a little shaky. He was right, of course. But that had been so long ago, in a different time. A few times, she'd wondered about their love. If they'd stayed together, would it have remained strong? Or would it have died out as they grew older?

"We were so young," Lindsey said. "What did we know about love then?"

She wanted to say more, but she didn't have it in her.

"I think the real problem was you knocking that lock out of my hands," Jack said.

Lindsey laughed, grateful for the break in the seriousness of the conversation. "As I recall, your hands were shaky."

"I was cold," Jack defended.

"You were terrified." It felt good to finally say that out loud.

"Maybe a little," Jack admitted. They both smiled.

"Well, we didn't believe in that lock stuff anyway, right?" Lindsey waited for Jack's response. She was the one who had started the lock idea, but he was the one who'd insisted they go through with it that day.

"You know, they cut off all of the locks on our bridge. In fact, on all the bridges except the Pont Neuf," Jack explained.

Lindsey was surprised. "Why?"

"The bridges date back to Napoleon. Apparently, the railings were collapsing under the weight of the locks. They became a hazard."

Lindsey couldn't believe it. She'd thought they would be there forever. "The hazard of love."

"Pont Neuf is next. And then Paris will be love lock-less," Jack said.

"Well, there is still one lock at the bottom of the Seine."

"Should we go dive for it?" Jack asked. Lindsey smiled, happy that he understood what would make her laugh.

"Dive for what?" a voice asked from behind Lindsey. Lindsey turned around to find that it was the Englishwoman she had run into the night before when she'd been searching for Alexa. "Did you lose your daughter again?" the woman asked.

Lindsey shook her head. "No. She's all right this time."

"Good morning, Mrs. Daltry," Jack said.

"Good morning, Jack. And you know very well it's Kathryn." She looked back and forth at the two of them. "I didn't realize you two were together."

"Oh, we're not," Lindsey said quickly.

"We were," Jack corrected.

"But we're not," Lindsey reiterated.

"So, where's your daughter this morning?" Kathryn asked.

"She's with him again," Lindsey said, referring to J.P.

"There is something about Paris," Kathryn said. "Well, I won't keep you two." She took a step away, but Jack held up a hand.

"Actually, I've got to get back to work. You sit here." He got up from his seat and offered it to Kathryn. "Ladies, I'll leave you two."

"Thanks for the crossword," Lindsey said.

"Two down is artichoke," Jack said before he turned to walk away.

Lindsey pointed to Jack's empty seat. "Join me, please."

Kathryn sat down. "Thank you." Her gaze followed Jack as he walked off toward the front desk. When he was out of earshot, she said to Lindsey, "He's turned this into such a charming place over the years. The first time I stayed here with my husband, it was just a hole in the wall."

Kathryn was married? Lindsey had thought she was single. "When was that?"

"My honeymoon. Forty years ago." Kathryn wore a reminiscent smile.

"And you're back to celebrate?" Lindsey hadn't yet seen her husband, but then, Kathryn hadn't yet seen Alexa, either.

"No. He died. It's been two years now," Kathryn said.

Lindsey sank in her seat. "I'm so sorry." She felt terrible that she associated Paris with someone she had met when she was young and was still upset about it, and here was someone who'd been traveling here for years with a man she never wanted to leave.

Returning to Paris had to be difficult for Kathryn.

"We came to Paris every anniversary. This is the first time I've been back since," Kathryn said. "I thought if I could just see everything again, I could hold on to the memories." She paused for a second. "It sounds silly, I know."

Lindsey shook her head. "It doesn't at all. It sounds like you had a wonderful marriage."

"We did," Kathryn replied. Her voice was steady, but Lindsey could see right through her brave smile. She knew what it was like to no longer have the person you loved the most beside you. She wanted to do something to ease Kathryn's pain.

Should she ask her to explore the city, or go to Notre Dame? No—she had a better idea. When Lindsey was at her lowest point, after the lock had dropped to the bottom of the river, she'd headed straight to Hugo's. That was exactly where they had to go.

"You know, I'm going to visit a friend's art studio. He's kind of an artist-slash-meddler. Would you like to come with me?" If anyone could bring light into someone's life, it was Hugo. He didn't even have to know what was wrong. He could sense when someone was down, and he instinctively knew how to bring them happiness.

"I wouldn't want to intrude," Kathryn said.

"Trust me, he's un-intrudable," Lindsey said. "You have to come."

Kathryn's mouth curved upward. "If you insist. I'll come."

Lindsey nodded. "Absolutely!"

The two ladies gathered their coats, left behind some euros, and headed for the door. Today would be an adventure for both of them, Lindsey thought. A time to forget the past and move forward.

Chapter Seven

Next?

ALEXA AND J.P. WEAVED THEIR way through the Sorbonne. That morning, they had stopped at a tiny bakery just off campus where they sipped lattes and split one of the best croissants Alexa had ever tasted. It was perfectly crisp on the outside and buttery soft on the inside, just the way she liked them. She made a note that when her mom was there with her, they'd have to get one together, only next time, she wouldn't be splitting it with anyone. The pastry was so good that Alexa wanted her own.

In fact, she'd wanted her own with J.P., but she'd demurred because she didn't want to look like the stereotypical supersize-me American. Being in France made her realize just how much her culture over-consumed, and she'd only been there two days. She couldn't even fathom what she would notice once she'd been there an entire semester.

After their morning snack, she and J.P. walked through the center of campus to get to the student affairs building. At the University of Connecticut, Alexa had spent most of her time at the student union where there was a movie theater and activities every Friday night. Here, she was surrounded by architectural wonders that had been around for centuries. She was completely in awe.

"I love it already," Alexa said as they exited one of the more famous buildings in the middle of campus. "The trellises, the gardens, the stonework. I can't get enough of this place." She observed every little piece of architecture on campus as if she'd never seen a university before in her life. J.P. grinned.

"What are you smiling for?" Alexa asked.

"You. You are like a kid in a candy shop. It's fun to watch you take this all in," J.P. said. "It gives me a new respect for the university."

"Really? That seems a little dramatic."

"It's not dramatic. It's just French passion. Come on, I'll show you the dorms. You're in the best one." J.P. grabbed her hand and led her to the east of the building they had just exited. After registering for their classes, he'd taken Alexa to find out where she was staying. She was in one of the oldest dorms that had recently been remodeled. Every room had vaulted ceilings and intricate woodwork. His best friend had lived in the same dorms during their first year at school, and J.P. told her he was always jealous of his friend's place.

Now J.P. lived in a small apartment off campus with his best friend and another roommate. He had promised Alexa he'd bring her to his place later, but for now, he was leading her around campus, showing her where she'd live for the next few months.

As they meandered through the expanse of the university, J.P. pointed to each building and gave a brief history. They'd already passed the physics department where Marie Curie had studied and the church where the Princess of Monaco was rumored to have prayed for better grades.

"The art department's over there," J.P. said, pointing to a large stone building with gargoyles around the top. Alexa liked the look of it.

"And where's the math department?" she asked.

J.P. pointed to another building. "It's just across the way."

"We can wave through the windows," Alexa said. As soon as the words were out of her mouth, she wondered if she was being too enthusiastic. They had known each other for only two days, and acting as if they'd be seeing each other every day was a tad bit presumptuous. "But I'm sure we'll both be super busy," she said.

"That's true."

They continued walking toward her dorm, but J.P. remained quiet, as though deep in thought. Was she scaring him off? She hadn't thought about him in any serious way. She simply liked spending time with him. And the idea of starting a new school with a familiar face on campus put her at ease.

"So, your mother went here?" he asked, finally breaking the silence.

Alexa was so deep in her own thoughts that it took her a moment to register that he'd asked about her mom. "Semester abroad, just like me." Alexa looked around at the opulent campus. "I can't believe she never came back."

"Well, she's here now," J.P. said.

"Yeah, she is," Alexa said.

"I'm glad she let you come away with me today. This has been incredibly fun." He grabbed her hand and walked her straight to the front of another magnificent building. "This," he started, "is where you'll be living."

Alexa gasped, staring up at the grand building of pale brick in an Art Deco style. "Are you serious?" J.P. nodded. "I've never lived somewhere this nice."

"Well, Paris has a lot of great things to

offer." He squeezed her hand a little tighter. Alexa smiled. Clearly, whatever *faux pas* she imagined she'd made earlier had made no impact on J.P.

"I'm so glad you offered to take me around today," Alexa said.

"Me too. I wish I could show you the inside, but the doors are locked for residents only."

"When I get my key, I'll show you inside."

"I'd like that," J.P. said and they walked away from the dorm and back through campus.

Across the city, Lindsey and Kathryn arrived at Hugo's studio.

"Are you sure he won't mind? This place looks serious," Kathryn said as they exited the elevator and the smell of fresh paint wafted through the air.

"I'm sure," Lindsey said. "Hugo loves company. He says it keeps him inspired."

"Well, I don't know how inspiring I'll be, but I love art." Kathryn straightened her blouse.

"Hugo's going to love you," Lindsey said, then opened the door to the studio.

Hugo was working on the same canvas he had been painting the day before. His back was to them as they entered. Lindsey shuffled her feet to get Hugo's attention.

"Lindsey!" Hugo exclaimed as he turned around. "And a friend," he finished when he saw Kathryn.

Kathryn beamed.

"Hugo Blanchett, this is Kathryn Daltry. Kathryn, this is the meddler," Lindsey said. Hugo extended his hand then moved in for the double-kiss hello. Kathryn followed suit.

"What a pleasure," Hugo said as he backed away from Kathryn.

"Your work is incredible," Kathryn said.

"About half the people who come here say the opposite."

"It's the other half you should listen to," Kathryn replied.

"If only you were an art critic," he said. "You're not a critic, are you?"

Lindsey cringed. She knew how much Hugo hated critics. In Hugo's opinion, the critics were the worst. They were fickle and constantly changed their minds. One year, his work would be magnificent, the next, subpar. It was part of the game of making a living from the arts, but it was still difficult to get used to.

"I'm just a tourist," Kathryn demurred.

Hugo winked. "I doubt that." He turned to Lindsey. "And how do you like your hotel?"

Lindsey wasn't even sure how to respond. She couldn't be mad because the hotel and their suite were fantastic, but on the other hand... "You could have mentioned it was Jack's."

His eyes twinkled. "I couldn't tell you it was Jack's. What would be the fun in that?"

Lindsey shook her head. "You haven't changed at all."

"Thank you." Hugo was clearly proud of his meddling skills. Lindsey wanted to be upset, but Hugo was one of those people that made it hard to stay mad. But she wished she'd at least had a warning before she ran into Jack at the bar. At least then she could've prepared herself a little better. She would've rehearsed what to say and not stumbled so much. Plus, she could've also been ready to explain the whole situation to Alexa, or given her fair warning that she had no clue what would happen if they ran into Jack.

"I haven't seen much of him over the years. But he's still single from what I hear," Hugo said.

"Stay out of it, Hugo," Lindsey said firmly.

Hugo smiled. "Okay, I will." He turned to Kathryn. "How long are you here for?"

"A few days," she said as Hugo looked her up and down. Kathryn squirmed.

"Just enough time for me to paint you," he said.

"Oh no, I couldn't."

"Give me one reason why not," Hugo said.

"I'm sure I could give you several," Kathryn muttered.

Lindsey could sense Kathryn's discomfort and stepped in. "Maybe another time, Hugo," she said.

Hugo shook his head. "Lindsey, if I've taught you nothing else, one must seize the moment. And the moment is here."

Lindsey knew the speech. It was the same one he'd given her when she started painting the love locks bridge. He was the one who'd encouraged her to bring up the idea of the lock to Jack.

Hugo turned to Kathryn. "Madame, it would be my honor. Perhaps just a quick sketch. For now."

Kathryn paused, then said to Hugo, "I suppose that would be all right."

Hugo clapped his hands together in excitement. "It's settled. Lindsey, will you gesso a canvas?"

Lindsey hesitated. She couldn't remember the last time she had primed a canvas. "I haven't done that in—"

"I know. Twenty years," Hugo said, then

turned to Kathryn. "She was my best student."

"He's prone to exaggeration," Lindsey said quickly. She didn't want to go down this road with Hugo.

"We'll never know now, will we?" Hugo asked. "Because you quit."

Lindsey flinched.

He handed her a paintbrush. "In case you've forgotten, this is a brush." He then pointed to an easel. "And that's a canvas. Is it all coming back to you now?"

Lindsey smiled. Despite the fact she knew Hugo was riding her, it felt good to be back under his tutelage. It felt even better to have a paintbrush in her hand. "Yes, *maestro*," she said as she got to work.

Hugo pulled out a chair for Kathryn and placed it in the middle of the room. "And you, my dear, may sit here." Kathryn eased onto the stool and sat up straight and stiff. Hugo placed his hands on her shoulders and gently pushed them down. Kathryn relaxed into a more easeful pose. "There. Beautiful," he said.

While Lindsey painted the canvas with the gesso primer, she watched the two of them interact. As far as Lindsey knew, Hugo had only had one love his entire life. She'd left him when he was in his twenties, and he'd never quite recovered. Instead of looking for something permanent, he'd thrown himself into his work and his students had become his children. Watching Hugo with Kathryn now, Lindsey couldn't help but wonder if there was a spark between them.

"I see in your eyes both a sadness and a joy. And I will capture both," Hugo said as he began sketching her image. Kathryn smiled.

Lindsey watched as Hugo continued sketching. When she finished the canvas, she placed it next to him. "I'm going to go. Do you need anything else?"

"Are you sure you don't want to stay? Maybe work on something of your own?" Hugo asked, barely lifting his head from the sketch.

Lindsey knew he was hinting at her finishing the painting of the love locks bridge.

"I'm sure. Alexa should be back soon, and I want to be there when she arrives. We're supposed to visit Notre Dame later," Lindsey said, lying. She and Alexa hadn't made any plans. She simply wanted to leave Hugo and Kathryn alone, and she hadn't checked in with the office since she'd arrived in Paris. "I'm going to go."

"Suit yourself," Hugo said.

"I'll see you later," Kathryn said.

"Absolutely. I'm sure we'll run into each other at the hotel," Lindsey said. "Enjoy your time here."

Kathryn nodded, then Lindsey left, leaving Hugo and Kathryn all alone.Outside, Lindsey realized that she, too, was all alone in Paris. Something she hadn't experienced since she'd arrived twenty years ago. After her first week in the city, it was Jack, then Hugo. Now it was Alexa, then Hugo, Jack, and Kathryn. But here she was, standing at the precipice of the wide-open metropolis, solo.

She took a deep breath and crossed the street. There was an extra spring in her step. She had forgotten how beautiful Paris was when you opened your eyes and simply observed. When there was no agenda, backstory, or thoughts of love.

She walked through the seventh *arrondissement* and made her way through to the Grand Palais des Champs-Élysées. The sight was more beautiful than she remembered. There were tourists and couples everywhere. The monument had been there for well over a hundred years. It stood as a reminder that though people come in and out of your life, some things remain the same. Lindsey sat down on a bench to people-watch when a couple on bicycles caught her eye.

The image brought her back to the days that she and Jack had spent traversing the city on two wheels. He was fond of packing his basket with picnic supplies every time they went biking. They would stop and eat at some of the quaintest places around Paris. When she thought about Jack, she didn't remember the late nights or the intimate moments, so much as the innocent moments, the ones that made her feel as if they could do this forever—that they belonged together.

Lindsey shook her head to release the thought. She didn't still believe she and Jack belonged together, did she? If that was true, they would've made it work years ago, right? *This was just a nice time of reflection on a great moment in the past.* In the same way that she missed the scent of newborn baby skin, she wouldn't trade anything to have Alexa back in diapers and operating on no sleep. She was fond of the memories, but that didn't mean she had to try to recreate them.

Lindsey watched as the couple on bikes rode off down the street and disappeared into the afternoon sun. She then got up from her bench and began the walk back to her hotel.

In her room, Lindsey checked her messages and emailed Maggie to see if there was any word from Trent. She had given more thought to the magazine. That was her present, not Jack. She didn't want to let it go, and she was hoping that Trent had forgotten about the fact that she was in Paris, a stone's throw away from London. She had enough to deal with on the trip, and the last thing she needed was an incredibly gorgeous man asking her to dinner so he could buy her company.

Lindsey was midsentence in her email response to Maggie when there was a knock at the door. "Coming!" she shouted.

She crossed through the living area and opened the door to find Jack standing with a beautiful arrangement of roses.

Her heartbeat sped up. "Wow," she said. Not her most articulate moment—but the sight of Jack with flowers left her totally flustered.

"These are for you," he said.

"They're beautiful. You shouldn't have." Lindsey reached for the bouquet. She was impressed by the gesture, but a little hesitant to take them since she was allergic to roses. She hadn't been around them in forever. Jack knew this, or so she'd thought. But then again, why would he remember that, after all this time?

"I didn't send these. They're from..." Jack looked at the card. "Trent Greer?"

Lindsey quickly grabbed the flowers. She didn't want to have to explain anything to Jack. "Thank you."

Jack stood in the doorway, watching as she brought them into her room. "I thought you were allergic to roses."

So he did remember. "Not anymore," Lindsey said. Let Jack think she had another man after her. If she couldn't have her moment of telling him he was too late, at least she could have this. "Are you waiting for a tip?"

"Nope, I'm good," Jack said, still smiling.

"Okay, well. Thanks again."

"Don't mention it," Jack said as Lindsey closed the door quickly.

She took two steps inside the room. "Ah-hhchooo!" She nearly dropped the flowers as she sneezed. She turned around to make sure the door was closed, but knew there was no way Jack hadn't heard her.

Chapter Eight

A Delicate Dance

LINDSEY PUT THE FLOWERS NEXT to Alexa's bed in the suite. Alexa loved roses, but because of Lindsey's allergy, they'd never had them in the house. The last time Lindsey had received the red flower was on her second date with Dane. He'd surprised her with them before a night out, and she'd surprised him with an allergy attack.

Jack had always known about her allergy. They were both in art history class together, and the professor had brought in a giant bouquet of roses. Lindsey sat in the front row. That day, she couldn't stop sneezing. She'd had to announce to the entire class that she was having a reaction to the roses and ask the professor to remove them. After class, Jack had approached her with a Kleenex and a Benadryl. "Do you always carry drugs?" Lindsey asked after she thanked him for coming to her rescue.

"Just antihistamines. There's one week every spring where the pollen is so intense around here that I can barely breathe. That's been in my backpack since April. But don't worry, it's still good," he'd said.

"Thank you," Lindsey said.

"So, it seems you'd be a pretty cheap girl," Jack had said.

Lindsey had stiffened at that. "Excuse me?"

"Sorry. I meant you'd be a cheap girl-friend, since no one could ever buy you roses," Jack had told her.

Lindsey had laughed at his terrible attempt at a joke, but still, she wasn't impressed. That is, until the next day when he showed up to class with a dozen tulips in the middle of fall.

"These aren't even in season," Lindsey had said. "They must've cost a fortune."

"Nah," Jack had said humbly. "I know a few people."

"Are you part of the flower mafia?" Lindsey had asked him, hoping that her attempt at a joke didn't turn out to be true.

"No, my dad's in the hotel business. There was a wedding last weekend, and the bride had these flown in from Holland."

"You stole them?"

"Don't worry, these were leftover. They

gave them to me. And now I'm giving them to you," Jack had said.

"They're beautiful. Thank you."

From then on, every time there was a wedding at his dad's hotel, Jack would bring Lindsey a bouquet of the most exotic and unattainable flowers imaginable.

As Lindsey closed the door to Alexa's room behind her, she smiled at the memory. She sat on her bed and wondered what Alexa and J.P. were doing. She imagined he was showing her the city and hoped Alexa was happy with her choice to move to France for the semester.

Exhausted, Lindsey laid her head down for a second.

When she woke up, she looked at her watch and realized it was already three o'clock. She'd taken a half hour nap, and she hadn't even eaten lunch yet. She put on a fresh coat of lipstick, fussed with her hair, then headed downstairs for a bite to eat.

As Lindsey entered the dining room, she saw Kathryn sitting at a table alone, sipping a cup of tea. She was curious how the session with Hugo had gone, so she walked over. Kathryn looked up as Lindsey approached.

Kathryn's face brightened. "Hello, dear. I was hoping to see you."

"How was your sitting with Hugo?" She had thought she sensed a connection between the two. Even if she were wrong about that, she knew how Hugo could make anyone feel special, and she'd hoped the afternoon had brightened Kathryn's trip to Paris.

"He's very opinionated," Kathryn muttered.

Lindsey nodded in agreement. "He is."

"And demanding," Kathryn said.

This wasn't telling Lindsey anything. "That, too."

"He wouldn't show me the sketch," Kathryn said.

Typical Hugo. "And he won't, until he's finished." Lindsey paused, then asked, "Are you going back?"

Kathryn shook her head. "I don't think so. But thank you for the introduction. If things were different, perhaps…"

Lindsey guessed that she was remembering a different time. A time when she was a young woman, perhaps?

"I shouldn't have come back here," Kathryn said as her head dropped.

Lindsey's heart pinched in sympathy as she sat down next to the older woman. She understood all too well. While Paris might be for lovers, it wasn't the place to reflect on lovers lost. "I've had those same thoughts. If it wasn't for my daughter, I probably wouldn't have come back." After a certain time, she'd had no need to seek revenge on Jack and no desire to figure out what had happened to him so long ago. Her past was her past, and she was happy to leave it there.

Kathryn looked at her with an all-knowing look. "You were in love in Paris."

"A long time ago," Lindsey confessed.

It was the first time she'd admitted she'd loved Jack since she'd returned to Paris.

"James and I had the best times here. Just walking and talking, nothing out of the ordinary. Yet somehow extraordinary."

Lindsey had never really experienced that kind of magic with her ex-husband. Was that what she and Jack would've shared, if they had never parted? "You're lucky to have had a love like that," she said.

Kathryn smiled. "I am." Lindsey could see her retreat to the corners of her mind where the memories of her husband were probably stored.

"I know we've just met," Lindsey began, "and I'm definitely no expert on love… but I can't help but think he'd want you to be happy again."

Kathryn looked up, and Lindsey hoped she hadn't overstepped her bounds.

"That's exactly what he'd want," Kathryn said. "If only I could."

The gravity of her statement hung in the air. Lindsey couldn't think of anything else to say.

Kathryn changed the subject. "And where's your lovely daughter?"

"She left this morning on the back of a Vespa. And she's not answering her phone." She'd tried to call Alexa several times. She'd even excitedly texted her a picture of the roses from Trent to entice her back to the hotel, but Alexa hadn't answered. Lindsey sighed.

"Here, have a cup of tea," Kathryn said as she handed Lindsey the small kettle of hot water. "She'll be back soon."

Lindsey selected a teabag from the tray in the middle of the table and poured the hot water into her mug. "I know I worry too much, but it's so hard not to."

"You're a mother. Occupational hazard," Kathryn comforted her. "I still worry about my children, and they're married with kids of their own."

"So it never stops?" Lindsey asked.

Kathryn shook her head. "Never."

Lindsey sipped her tea and wondered where Alexa and J.P. had ended up.

"Are you sure your mom won't mind? Shouldn't you check in with her?" J.P. asked as they climbed onto a hop-on, hop-off tour boat on the Seine.

On campus, J.P. had showed her all the best places for coffee and food. He'd also pointed out the secret book stacks in the main library and admitted he'd always dreamed of kissing someone there one day. In that moment, Alexa had frozen. As much as she was enjoying her time with J.P., she wasn't quite ready for the first kiss. After all, they hadn't known each other for long.

Maybe J.P. had sensed her reluctance, because he'd told her another fact about the library, and they'd kept on walking.

After they had explored the entire campus, Alexa had asked J.P. to show her more of Paris. Even though it was a totally touristy thing to do, J.P. had suggested the boat tour. It was one of his favorite things to do in the afternoon.

"I'm eighteen. It's fine. I don't need to call her," Alexa said as she found a seat toward the back of the boat where she could look down the river and see the Eiffel Tower. "I'm having fun."

J.P. shrugged his shoulders.

After her tea and a small sandwich, Lindsey went back to her room to wait for Alexa. She had bought several art magazines from the stand down the street and had been flipping through them, getting inspiration for *POV*.

She circled layouts and folded the corners of the pages to mark all the things that she wanted to do once she returned home. Or should do, anyway. Her heart wasn't completely in it, even though her entire bed was covered in glossy paper.

After a couple of hours, Alexa still hadn't returned or answered her phone, and Lindsey started to get worried. She looked out the window where the sun was beginning to set, but there was no sign of her daughter.

She gathered up the magazines and neatly placed them inside her computer case for safekeeping. As she was zipping up her bag, there was a knock on the door. *Finally, she's back.*

Without even looking through the peephole, she flung the door wide open. "Where have you been?" she demanded but then paused when she realized the person standing in front of her wasn't Alexa, but Jack.

"Folding towels?" Jack joked.

Lindsey sighed. "I thought you were Alexa."

Jack looked at his watch. "She's not back yet?"

Lindsey picked up her phone and dialed Alexa once more. "And not answering her cell."

"I'm happy to call J.P. for you," Jack offered.

Lindsey exhaled in relief. "Thank you. That would be amazing."

Jack pulled his phone out of his pocket, scrolled through his contacts, and hit call. Lindsey waited as the phone rang. Jack put it on speakerphone, but the call went to voice mail. Jack left a message. "J.P., it's Jack. I'm with Alexa's mom. We're just wondering where you two are. Give me a call when you get a chance. Thanks."

"That's it?" Lindsey asked after Jack hung up the phone.

His eyes glinted in amusement. "What'd you want me to do, tell him he was grounded?"

"Yes. No. Sorry, I'm just worried."

"I'm sure they lost track of time," Jack assured Lindsey, but she was anything but assured.

"How long have you known this J.P. kid?"

"He's worked here a couple months."

"That's all?" Lindsey asked.

"He's a good guy."

"How do you know?"

"J.P.'s a good kid," he repeated. "He works hard, shows up on time, and makes all the guests feel welcome. Plus, he's a math major, how dangerous could he be?"

Lindsey smiled. Jack had a point. And even though part of her resisted the idea, she knew that Alexa was old enough to be out on her own.

"Come on, let's take a walk," Jack said. "You need to get out of this room. We could go look for them."

He was right. Paris was one of the most beautiful cities in the world, and she shouldn't waste it staying cooped up in her hotel room. And if they happened to find Alexa and J.P., so much the better. She grabbed her coat.

"Now, where would two young people in love go?" Jack asked as they headed down the stairs.

Lindsey followed close behind, pulling her arms through the sleeves of her jacket. "In love? They met yesterday." There was no way Alexa and J.P. could be in love already. That was impossible.

"Hey, how long did it take us?" Jack asked.

Lindsey's stomach flipped. He had a point. After the day he'd brought her the tulips, they'd been inseparable for the rest of the semester.

"That was different," Lindsey said. *We were older.*

"If you say so," Jack said with a smile.

"This is not good. It can only end one way." Lindsey followed him into the bar area, shaking her head.

"So, if something ends, that means it

shouldn't have started?" Jack asked as he grabbed his coat from behind the bar.

"I just don't want her to go through what we went through," Lindsey said as Jack turned to her and put on his coat. Part of her hated talking about it, but another part of her felt relieved to get it out in the open.

"But we were happy."

Lindsey paused before she followed him. He was right. "We were," she said, "but that was only a few months." And the time after that hadn't been happy for her at all.

"I'll give you that," Jack said as they approached the front door of the hotel. "But still… wasn't it worth it?" He winked.

Lindsey had to nod. The time they'd spent together was amazing, but she also couldn't erase the fact that the year that followed her return to New York had been hell. She didn't want to watch Alexa go through the same thing.

Jack held the door for her as they exited the building. Lindsey was so caught up in her thoughts that she didn't even thank Jack. "You're welcome," he muttered.

"Sorry," Lindsey said. "I'm distracted. I know she's an adult and can make her own decisions. I just don't want to see her hurt."

"I get that," Jack said. "I doubt any parent wants to see their kid in pain."

Lindsey smiled. Jack always had a way

to calm her in the tensest situations. When she'd had to turn in her mid-semester project, he'd carried her five by eight canvas from Hugo's all the way to the art department on campus. The entire walk over, he'd regaled her with tales of Paris to distract her. Lindsey needed that same thing right then and there. "Tell me something else," she said. "I need to stop worrying."

"So Trent Greer of Greer Publishing, offices in New York, Los Angeles, London, and Paris," Jack said changing the subject.

Lindsey stared at him. How did he know so much?

"Google," Jack said.

"You're Googling my roses?" Despite the fact that she had yet to go out on a date with Trent, she liked the idea of Jack thinking there was something going on between them. She didn't want to tell him all the details.

"Yep. I Googled your roses. Why didn't he know you were allergic?"

Jack had her there. She couldn't cover that fact up. "He wants to buy my magazine," she admitted.

"So, they're business roses?" Jack smirked. He looked way too pleased about this.

"I'm pretty sure," Lindsey said. Though Trent had asked her out on a date back in

New York, so maybe there was something more. "I don't know."

"Well, it seems like he probably knows. Also, if they're more than 'business,' you might want to tell him you're allergic. Save the guy some money."

Lindsey tilted her head. "I see your point."

Jack and Lindsey crossed the street to the Quai des Tuileries and walked down the steps to the walkway that wound along the Seine. The winter sun was out, and people filled the area. It wasn't too crowded, but it was perfect. Lindsey took in the sights and sounds around them. Two women passed, complaining about how their husbands never folded the laundry, a young girl sat on a bench, reading *Jane Eyre*, and an elderly man sketched on his easel overlooking the water.

She and Jack had walked this path at least once a week when they were younger. It was their Friday afternoon ritual. They'd get out of class and meet at Lindsey's dorm. From there, they'd bike to the river walkway entrance closest to school. They'd lock up their bikes and walk for hours, talking and laughing. It wasn't extraordinary, but it was theirs.

"Remember that picnic we had here?"

Lindsey asked as they passed by a small park.

"Ants and a thunderstorm?" Jack recalled.

Lindsey nodded and they both smiled. Back then, it was as if nothing else mattered. They could be soaking wet with ants covering their cheese, and they still found something beautiful in the moment. Their relationship had always been easy.

"What was your husband like?" Jack asked, interrupting her train of thought.

"Pretty much the opposite of you," Lindsey replied. Dane was a financial analyst. He was eight years older than Lindsey and ready to settle down when she'd met him.

"Ouch," Jack said.

His tone was light, but she could see that he was genuinely hurt. "I think I just didn't want to be reminded of you. Or us. Anyway, that didn't last long."

"I'm sorry." Jack seemed sincere.

"Thanks," Lindsey said, "but that's almost as old news as us. And I got Alexa out of it, so I'm grateful for that."

"As you should be," Jack said.

After she and Dane divorced, her focus had gone directly into Alexa and later, the magazine. "I'm going to go out on a limb here and guess you never said 'I do?'" Lindsey pried.

Jack shook his head. "I did not."

"Still dodging that commitment, huh?" Lindsey said, unable to help herself.

"I committed," Jack said. "To a hotel."

Lindsey smiled. "Well, you two do seem very happy together."

"We have our ups and downs. Like any relationship."

Lindsey knew exactly what he was talking about. She'd had her highs and lows with the magazine, too.

A fresh thought struck her. What if her and Jack's twenty years apart was just a down time?

She brushed the idea aside. Twenty years was twenty years. They continued reminiscing as they made their way down the river.

As the sunlight dimmed, they finished their walk at the Seine terrace. Jack directed her over to an area where a bunch of people were gathered. A man at one of the bistro tables had a boom box on a chair that played tango music. Couples danced all around the outdoor park area.

"What are we doing here? You know I don't dance," Lindsey said, turning to Jack.

"Oh, I know. We're just here to watch." Jack gently placed his hand on her cheek and directed her eyes back to the dancing couples.

"Voilà!" Jack said.

Lindsey looked at the dancers. There, in the middle of it all, were J.P. and Alexa.

Lindsey's mouth fell open. "How did you know they'd be here?"

"J.P. teaches tango on Monday nights," Jack said matter-of-factly.

"You could've told me that."

"Yeah. I could have," Jack said.

Lindsey shook her head and turned back to watch Alexa and J.P. dance. J.P. was a good teacher. Alexa seemed to know all the steps and had no problem letting him lead. When Alexa had been younger, her report cards had always commented on the fact that she was "bossy." Lindsey used to take that to mean that her daughter had strength and knew what she wanted, but later, when Alexa had gotten into high school, Lindsey understood that her daughter couldn't be told what to do.

Though Alexa had gotten over her rebellious teenage years quickly, Lindsey still worried sometimes. The world wasn't kind to "bossy" women. However, seeing her now with J.P. made her smile. Alexa had a perfect balance of letting go of control and being in charge.

Lindsey watched as J.P. twirled Alexa and grabbed her close. Then, as the music hit a dramatic beat, he wrapped his arm around the small of her back and dipped her.

Alexa was completely in the moment until she opened her eyes and found herself looking straight up at her. "Mom?!"

"Hi, Alexa," Lindsey said.

J.P. guided Alexa upright and Alexa broke free and marched straight to her mother. "This is so embarrassing," she muttered.

"You weren't answering your phone," Lindsey pointed out. "I didn't know where you were."

"My battery's dead."

"I'm sorry, madame. We lost track of time," J.P. said as he approached.

Lindsey couldn't help but notice how innocent he looked. She knew they hadn't meant to worry her. "It happens," she said.

Alexa smiled at her mom. *Thank you.* Lindsey nodded, then turned to J.P. "Where did you learn to tango?"

"My grandfather's from Argentina. But when he and my grandmother divorced, he moved here," J.P. explained.

"And lost his dance partner?" Lindsey asked, picturing J.P.'s grandfather teaching J.P. to dance because he no longer had a wife and he needed someone to dance with.

"He lost *all* his dance partners." J.P. smiled. "That's why he and my grandmother divorced."

Jack clapped his hands together and laughed. As the music started up again, he held out his hand to Lindsey.

"No way," Lindsey protested, trying to get away from Jack's advance.

"Yes way," Jack said as he took control of the situation and interlaced his fingers with Lindsey's and wrapped his other arm around her lower back. In true tango style, he straightened their front arms, pressed his cheek to hers, and led her to the middle of the dance floor.

They dramatically stumbled through the first steps. They were not good dancers, but they were good partners. They couldn't stop laughing as Jack twisted and twirled Lindsey. Alexa and J.P. stood off to the side, watching.

"They're pretty good," Lindsey heard J.P. say.

"No, they're not," Alexa said.

"I didn't mean their dancing. I meant they're pretty good together," he said. Out of the corner of her eye, Lindsey saw Alexa nod in agreement.

When the sun slipped farther down the horizon and the afternoon cooled into night, Lindsey, Jack, Alexa, and J.P. made their way back to the hotel.

Alexa filled Lindsey in on the day's ad-

ventures while J.P. ribbed Jack for his dancing skills.

"Okay, so my footwork's a little off," Jack
said as they got to the front of the hotel.

"A little?" Lindsey questioned with a
smile.

"I may be older, but I still have moves,"
Jack said as J.P. held the door open for everyone.

As they passed a couple on their way
out, Jack grabbed Alexa's hand and twirled
her into the entrance of the bar.

"He's not bad, Mom," Alexa said as she
came out of the move. Lindsey just shook her
head. She was about to say more when their
entire conversation was interrupted by a tall
brunette who stood up from the bar.

"Jack, there you are," the woman said as
she walked up to Jack and held his hands in
a familiar manner. "You promised to take me
to dinner."

Jack's face went into a wide grin. Lindsey
noticed. It was a mask of sorts. "Was that
tonight?"

"No, it wasn't tonight, but I'm here," the
woman said playfully as she slipped her arm
around Jack's.

Lindsey watched the entire exchange
with a smiling mask of her own.

"Lindsey and Alexa, this is Nicole," Jack
said.

"His girlfriend," Nicole quickly added.

Lindsey's perma-grin got bigger as did Jack's. "So nice to meet you," she said.

"And how are you enjoying our city?" Nicole asked, drawing even closer to Jack.

"You know what they say. A bad day in Paris is still better than a good day anywhere else," Lindsey said without thinking, then kicked herself mentally because that was more awkward than her favorite line from her favorite movie, *Dirty Dancing*. *I carried a watermelon.*

"How charming," Nicole said with an insincere smile.

The awkwardness between the two women was palpable. Alexa quickly grabbed her mother's arm. "C'mon, Mom. We've got that thing."

"Right. We have a thing," Lindsey agreed. "Nice to meet you, Nicole. Thanks for the day, Jack," Lindsey said as she and Alexa walked off toward the stairs to the elevator.

Lindsey and Alexa rode the elevator in silence. When they got inside their room, Lindsey went straight to the balcony and stood out under the stars. Alexa walked out and weaved her arm through her mother's. "You okay?" she asked.

"Of course I'm okay. Why wouldn't I be?" She doubted she was fooling Alexa.

"I was just checking."

"Now look who's worrying about who," Lindsey said. This was why she'd never told Alexa about Jack or seldom brought the men she dated around her. She never wanted Alexa to worry.

"You guys looked so cute dancing," Alexa said.

"You said we looked terrible."

"But you were terrible together," Alexa said wistfully.

"Well, we're not together." Lindsey stood next to her daughter, looking out over the Seine to the Eiffel Tower in the distance. That was the truth. She and Jack weren't together yesterday or the day before, and they certainly weren't together now.

"Look at that," Alexa said as she pointed to the twinkling lights on the Eiffel Tower and changed the subject.

"The City of Lights."

"The City of Love," Alexa said as she leaned her head on her mom's shoulder.

"Let's stick with lights," Lindsey said. How can a city be of something if that something is never stable? Love isn't forever, but light is. Light bulbs can be changed. Electricity can be wired into the dark parts. Love, on the other hand, is finite. It can't always be fixed and it can't always be found.

"Okay, it's the City of Lights." Alexa reached into her pocket and pulled out a wrapped piece of chocolate. "And the best chocolate ever."

Alexa broke the chocolate in half and handed a piece to Lindsey.

"Well, we'll always have chocolate," Lindsey said and popped it into her mouth, then wrapped her arm around her daughter.

Lindsey let her chocolate melt slowly in her mouth. "I hope it doesn't go by too fast," Alexa said.

"It will." Lindsey looked out at the lights of the city. "It always does."

Chapter Nine

The City of Lights (not love)

THE NEXT MORNING, LINDSEY WOKE up with a new determination. She no longer wanted to be distracted by Jack. She wanted to enjoy all the city had to offer. Her goal was to spend the last few days in Paris with her daughter and Hugo.

"I have our entire day planned," Lindsey said as she grabbed a croissant from the basket in front of her. She and Alexa were at breakfast in the hotel. J.P. was working the morning shift in the dining room and was extremely attentive to their table. He'd refilled their coffees twice and brought an extra basket of croissants, muffins, and pastries.

"I'd expect nothing else. I can't wait to explore with you." Alexa took a bite of her pastry.

"We'll start with the Place du Tertre." Lindsey's excitement rose. It was one of her favorite places in the entire world. Artists lined the plaza with easels—painting, sketching, and selling their work. In fact, Lindsey used to set up her own easel there. She'd never sold anything, but the energy in the place had inspired her to keep painting. In the corner, she noticed Jack serving another table and trying to listen to their conversation.

"Maybe we should invite Jack," Alexa said. Jack perked up at the mention of his name and moved a little closer to their table.

"Nah. He's seen it all," Lindsey said with her eyes on Jack as he approached their table.

"Yes, I have," Jack said, then turned to J.P., who had arrived with another basket of treats. "You might want to save a few pastries for the other guests."

J.P. nodded sheepishly and walked off. Alexa watched him go with a smiling gaze. Jack stood over their table with a tray of croissants in hand.

"So, ladies... how was your evening?" he asked.

Lindsey pasted on a smile. "Good. And dinner with Nicole?"

Jack turned away then looked at the croissants in his hand. "Dinner's dinner," he said. Lindsey could tell he wanted to change the subject. "Would you like another croissant?" he asked.

"No, you're saving those for the other guests, remember?" Lindsey pointed out.

"Right," Jack said, then started to walk off. He made it three steps before he turned back around. Alexa's eyes darted from him to Lindsey.

"Just for the record, she's not actually my 'girlfriend.' It's casual," Jack said when he was back in front of their table.

"Okay," Lindsey said. She didn't completely buy the story, but she did take some satisfaction in watching him squirm.

"Yeah… we've only been going out for a few weeks," he said firmly, then paused for a few seconds. "Or a little longer."

"It's cas," Lindsey said, shortening the word *casual.*

"Yes. It's casual." Jack shifted from one foot to the other as if he was going to walk away, yet he couldn't seem to move farther than two feet.

"Because you're committed to your hotel," Lindsey pointed out.

"Correct." They both smiled. Alexa looked at him, then her mother. Lindsey gave her a side smile. "Okay, I'm going to go," Jack said.

Lindsey nodded. After Jack walked off, Alexa turned to her.

"So…" Alexa started.

"So, after the Place du Tertre, I thought we'd see the Louvre," Lindsey said.

"*Mom.*"

"You won't believe how small the *Mona Lisa* is," Lindsey went on.

"Are we not going to talk about this whole Jack thing?" Alexa pointed over her shoulder.

"No. Because I'm here for you. And that's the only reason. Besides, there's no 'Jack thing' to talk about," Lindsey said, reaffirming the commitment she'd made to herself that morning.

J.P. inched closer to their table. "Speaking of which," Alexa began, "could you be a little less *here* for me?" She nodded at J.P. Lindsey turned around to see what she was looking at and understood immediately.

"Okay, maybe a little," she said as J.P. placed a fresh glass of orange juice on their table. Alexa nearly glowed as she thanked him. The innocent sight of the two of them making eyes at each other made Lindsey soften and she had an idea. "J.P., if you're free tomorrow, we'd like to invite you to an art show."

J.P. smiled. "I'm totally free."

"I thought you might be," Lindsey said.

J.P. grinned at Alexa. She smiled back, then turned to her mom and mouthed the words *thank you*. Lindsey was glad to see her daughter so happy.

After breakfast, the women walked to the eighteenth *arrondissement*. The cobblestone streets were flanked by cafés and shops. Locals and tourists mingled throughout the busy area.

"This is just like I pictured," Alexa said as they walked through the artists' stalls.

"It hasn't changed at all," Lindsey said as she looked around. She even recognized several artists who used to paint there when she was in school. They were grayer now, and a little rougher around the edges, but they were the same artists.

Lindsey led Alexa over to one of the familiar artists' stalls. She wanted to have their sketch done. Lindsey made a deal with the artist in French, and they sat down in the chairs across from him.

"Did you come here a lot?" Alexa asked.

"All the time," Lindsey said. "I used to come here and paint."

"Maybe one day, I'll set up here, too," Alexa said.

"That'd be great," Lindsey said. "But hold that thought. I have to find out something." She had to know more about the artist who was sketching them.

"Excuse *moi*," Lindsey said to the artist, then asked him if he remembered a young female artist with a pink easel. "I used to come here a long time ago."

The artist looked up from his sketch and stared at her. "*Oui*. I remember. Pink easel.

The young artist behind it, she wanted to paint all of Montmartre," the artist said with a big gesture of his hands. "We artists are just children who refuse to lay down their crayons, no?" the artist said.

"Oui," Lindsey said sadly, even though she had laid down her crayons.

"Your work, it was beautiful," the artist said.

"Thank you," Lindsey said. "Yours, too."

Lindsey felt a sense of nostalgia being recognized for her work. People used to notice her art; now it was the other way around. She was constantly recognizing others' works in her magazine or talking up Alexa's talents to her friends, but she never talked about her own paintings.

They sat still as the artist finished their sketch. All the while, Lindsey's mind wandered. She thought about what painting meant to her. In the beginning, it had been the only thing she could think of. It was her first love. Then there was Jack. Then there was the return to New York and the reality of life. Then the idea of making it as a painter dwindled, and Lindsey had to live in the real world, but even so, she kept the dream alive in her daughter.

When Alexa was five, Lindsey bought her a toy easel. When Alexa's teachers began to encourage her work, Lindsey knew Alexa had caught the bug. She'd been painting ever since.

Art was life.

Hugo stood in front of a large canvas filling in the sketch of Kathryn with paint. Ever since she'd left his studio, he hadn't been able to get her out of his mind. The sketch and the subsequent portrait had become his priority.

His palette was filled with warm colors he had specially mixed for the work. His hope was to finish it by the time of his showing. As he was painting, he heard footsteps. *Lindsey*, he thought, but then he looked up and saw it was Kathryn. He put down his brush and palette and walked over to her.

"Kathryn. I wasn't sure you'd come back," he said.

She approached timidly. "I wasn't going to. But something Lindsey said made me change my mind."

"Well, I'm charming when you get to know me," Hugo said in a nonchalant manner that seemed to put her at ease, since she smiled. "Whatever she said, I'm glad you're back. I was just working on your portrait." Hugo gestured to the easel and the canvas.

Kathryn walked toward it. "Can I have a look?" she asked.

Hugo reached out and gently grabbed

her arms and turned her back toward him. "No. No. No. You can see it at the show." He sat her down on a stool.

Kathryn leaned back and took a deep breath. "You're putting it in a show? You can't be serious."

"Yes. Tomorrow. You come?" Hugo walked back to the easel and picked up his brush and paints.

"Actually, I was planning on leaving tomorrow," Kathryn said.

"So soon?" Hugo asked, genuinely concerned. They had only just met, but he was surprised by how much he wanted her to see the portrait when it was finished.

"I really only came to see it all again," Kathryn said wistfully.

"Oh, you've seen it all?" Hugo asked. Surely, she hadn't seen everything.

"Well, there is one more place," she began.

"Yeah?" Hugo asked.

"Pont Neuf."

"Pont Neuf? The last love locks bridge," he said.

"I hear they're cutting off the locks," Kathryn said, disappointment in her voice.

"Yes. Tragic." Hugo dipped his brush in paint and swept it over the canvas.

Kathryn sat silent for a moment as Hugo continued to paint. He could sense she wanted to say more but wasn't quite ready. He gave her the space to talk, and after a few moments, she began.

"Fifteen years ago," she said, "James surprised me with an antique lock. Heart-shaped. Inscribed with our names."

Hugo looked at her, but remained silent. He could tell this was hard for her.

"We were probably the oldest couple on that bridge." Kathryn took another deep breath. It was clear to Hugo she hadn't told anyone about the lock in years. "I thought I'd try to find it and bring it back with me," she said, then looked at Hugo. "It's silly, I know."

Hugo shook his head. He understood her sentiment and her plan. "It's not silly. We must go," he said and put down his brush and paint.

"Now?" Kathryn asked.

"Yes, now," Hugo insisted as he helped her off the stool.

"But surely it would be a fool's errand."

"Well, then you've got the right man for the job." Hugo removed his painting coat and walked to the rack that held his jacket and scarf. "We'll go and we'll find it."

Kathryn stood back. "No. It doesn't matter."

"Well, it matters to you," Hugo said as he placed his red scarf around his neck. "And besides, I have a confession to make." He swung his jacket around his back and put it on.

"Let me guess. You have a lock hanging there, too," Kathryn said.

"The love of my life," Hugo said. "But it was not meant to be." He shrugged.

"I'm sorry," Kathryn said.

"The time we had was short. But it was magic," Hugo explained. It was a young love that didn't last. "So, how long did you and your James have together?" Hugo placed his hand on the back of her arm and led her out the door.

"My whole life."

"I envy you both," Hugo said, and he truly meant it.

"I miss us both," Kathryn said sadly.

"And that's why we must go and find your lock," Hugo said with a flare of determination.

They headed out the door and to the bridge.

After a day of shopping and sightseeing, Lindsey and Alexa returned to the hotel. Their hands were full of bags, and they both walked with a lightness to their step. It had been a good day in the city, just the two of them, exactly how Lindsey had wanted it.

As they walked to the front door, an

older couple exited the hotel. Lindsey smiled at them, then noticed that outside the front door were two bicycles. One had a picnic basket with a baguette popping out from inside. Lindsey paused at the sight. The bikes reminded her of hers and Jack's when they were younger. It was almost as if she had just finished class and Jack was there waiting to take her on their Friday night ritual around the city.

"What is it, Mom?" Alexa asked.

"Nothing," Lindsey said. Surely, the bikes had to be for some other guests. There was no way Jack had planned a ride for them.

The mother-daughter team walked through the open hotel door. J.P. was on the other side, holding it open.

"*Bonjour*," they said to him as they passed.

J.P. closed the door and turned in their direction. "Madame, I am on lunch break. May I take you and Alexa to the café?"

Both women turned and looked at him. "Oh, that's so sweet. But my mom and I have plans," Alexa said.

"Thank you, though," Lindsey said, impressed. Boys in America had never offered to take her to lunch when they took out her daughter.

"Of course, another time," J.P. said as he turned and walked out the door.

Lindsey thought for a moment, then turned to Alexa. "You know what? You two should go."

"No," Alexa said.

"Yes," Lindsey insisted as she placed her hand on Alexa's arm. They'd had an amazing day, she didn't need to monopolize all of Alexa's time. "I have to call Maggie in the office anyway."

Alexa paused. "Are you sure?"

"Yes, positive, go," Lindsey said.

Alexa smiled and handed her bags to her mom. "Thank you! And don't worry, my phone's charged!" she said as she took off for the door.

Lindsey watched her leave, then walked toward the steps to the elevator. As she approached them, Jack came out from the entranceway carrying a tray of glasses for the bar.

"How was sightseeing?" he asked.

"Sightseeing was great," Lindsey said and walked toward him. "And we did this." She put down her bags and started to unroll the sketch of her and Alexa. Of all the things in her shopping bags, it was the one thing Lindsey thought Jack would appreciate.

"What do you have here?" Jack asked as he set down the glasses. Lindsey held out the sketch. The Eiffel Tower was behind her and Alexa in the painting. Jack immediately recognized the work.

"The cat guy is still there?" Jack asked.

Lindsey was surprised. She'd hoped Jack would recognize the work, but didn't expect him to remember so quickly. She nodded. "Yes. The cat guy is still there."

Jack smiled. "This is great. You two will have this forever."

"I don't know about that," Lindsey said, "but it was fun. We had a good time together today."

Jack rolled up the sketch and handed it back to her. "Hey, I left a couple bikes out there, if you wanted to show Alexa the old route."

"Oh. Thanks, but she's gone off with J.P.," Lindsey said.

Jack put another glass away. "Again?"

Lindsey shrugged. What could she do?

"Am I going to have to put that guy on a double shift?" Jack asked.

"Could you?" Lindsey joked.

"I could, but that wouldn't be nice, now would it?"

"True, but it'd make me worry less." Lindsey smiled.

"Come on, give me a hand," Jack said, then started walking toward the door.

Lindsey followed Jack outside to the bikes. "Thank you, Jack. This was very thoughtful." She found it sweet that he'd remembered their old route, and also that he wanted her to share it with Alexa.

Jack started to move one of the bikes. "That's me," he said. "Monsieur Thoughtful. Help me take these bikes inside in case you and Alexa want to take them out later." He pushed one toward the door, but Lindsey stood in front of him. She had another idea.

"Or we could go. Now." Lindsey nervously clenched her fists as she waited for Jack to respond. Even though she had made the commitment to make the rest of her days in Paris about her daughter, she couldn't help herself. Riding bikes through the city and stopping to picnic were some of her favorite memories with Jack.

"We?" Jack asked as he pointed back and forth between them.

"Oui," she said with a hopeful smile.

Jack leaned the bike against the wall. "You know what? Just give me a second. I got to make a quick phone call," he said as he headed inside.

Lindsey happily grabbed the other bike and watched him walk away. She had always thought they'd ride together once more, but in her mind, it was supposed to happen in New York. However, a ride in Paris wasn't something she could pass up.

A few minutes later, Jack came back

outside and grabbed the other bike. "You ready?"

Lindsey's heart felt light. "Absolutely."

Together, they rode around the city. Through the Boulevard du Palais, past Notre Dame, and into the Cour Carrée. It was as if time stood still and Lindsey had never gone back to New York. On bikes, they were twenty-somethings again, absorbing the sights and laughing in each other's company.

Eventually, they made their way to the front of the Musée de l'Orangerie. In the past, they would stop here, eat a snack from their basket, and go inside and observe the paintings.

"We're here," Jack said.

"What do you mean?" Lindsey asked. They hadn't made a plan for the day. They were simply out for a ride.

"Leave the bikes there. They'll be fine," Jack said as he got off his and gathered the picnic basket.

"You sure?"

"Yeah," Jack said as he walked up the steps to the museum.

"Jack, isn't it closed?" The front door was shut behind a gilded wrought-iron gate.

"Come on," he said as he motioned her up the steps with the baguette in his hand.

"What have you got up your sleeve?"

Lindsey asked as they reached the top of the stairs.

Jack took a deep breath, then pushed on the heavy golden gate. The door slowly opened and he and Lindsey entered.

Once inside, Jack led her to a room that housed a painting of clouds that reflected on a water lily pond. It was a Monet they had both admired years ago. The museum was empty and their footsteps echoed throughout. Jack placed the picnic basket on the bench and gestured for Lindsey to take a seat.

She sat down and observed the painting that spanned the entire wall. "I won't even ask how you made this happen."

"Let's just say I have friends in low places."

"Hmmm, so nothing's changed."

"Nope." Jack pulled a chunk of bread from the baguette and took a bite.

"The first time we came here, you thought Monet was a champagne," Lindsey remembered.

"It isn't?" Jack said, chewing his bread. Lindsey shook her head.

"Thank you for bringing me here. You know it was always so crowded before, I never really saw these fully."

"It's all part of the Paris experience," Jack

said as he gestured to the painting in front of them and the two to the sides of them.

"Do you do this for all your guests?" Lindsey joked.

"Of course. Later this afternoon, I'll be closing down the Louvre for a Ping-Pong tournament," he said. Lindsey laughed. "No, come on," he said. "I never brought a guest back here." Jack paused for a moment. "Actually, I've never brought anyone back here."

"I'm honored," Lindsey said as he sat silently and stared at her. "What?" Lindsey asked, breaking the silence.

"Nothing," he said. She gave him a look. This was a moment they hadn't shared in years.

"Just looking at you. I, uh, I wanted to say three words," Jack said slowly.

"What three words?" Lindsey asked skeptically.

Jack hesitated, then said, "Ooh la la."

Lindsey laughed. She was relieved he hadn't said anything else, yet she was slightly disappointed. They sat in the moment of silence, neither saying a word.

"Life is the art of drawing without an eraser," Jack said in a contemplative tone and broke the silence.

"Who said that?" Lindsey asked.

"You did."

Lindsey had no recollection of that moment. "What? If I said that, I was probably just quoting Hugo or something," Lindsey said.

"Well, it stayed. And, uh, I made a few decisions I wish I could erase," he said.

"Who hasn't had those?" Lindsey said, attempting nonchalance. She wasn't sure she wanted to get into their entire past.

Jack's face got serious as he looked into Lindsey's eyes. "What happened to those two people that were us?"

"Life, I guess." Twenty years later she could see that that was true.

Jack looked at the painting, reflecting on the image. "I thought for sure I'd be married by now. A couple kids. A dog. Maybe two."

Lindsey was surprised. She always pictured Jack as someone who never wanted to settle down. "Really?"

"Yeah. One day. But 'one day' never happened."

"Yet," Lindsey said. "Maybe you're placing too much expectation on 'one day.'" If there was anything Lindsey had learned about love, it was to be a realist. There was no fantasy or perfect happy ending.

Jack shook his head. "It's your fault, you know. You're a hard act to follow."

Lindsey thought for a minute. His comment was sweet but didn't ring true to her.

"Well, obviously not that hard, because you didn't follow me," she said.

Jack raised his eyebrows. "Where's that eraser when you need it?"

Lindsey sat with that statement. What if they could've erased their past and done it over again? How would their lives have turned out? Even if Jack had come to New York, there was no guarantee they'd still be together today. Lindsey knew that now. But she also wished they'd had a chance to see what could've been.

Lindsey looked at Jack, an ache of longing in her chest. She was about to say more, but they were interrupted by a low voice.

"Monsieur, madame," a security guard said as he entered the room and pointed at his watch.

"Yeah, okay," Jack said quickly, got up, and began to pack their basket. "We got to go," Jack said as he gathered their things. "They're going to wax the floors." Jack hurried toward the door, but Lindsey hung back for a second and took one last look at the Monet. It was more powerful than she remembered.

Jack and Lindsey rode back to the hotel, reminiscing as they passed by each corner. While they hadn't shared the moment in the way Lindsey had always expected they would, they had come to a place of peace.

As they pulled up to the hotel laughing, Lindsey almost ran into a guest who was exiting a Mercedes taxi. She put her feet down onto the asphalt and attempted to squeeze by, but the man grabbed her shoulder.

"Lindsey?" She turned around to find that the voice belonged to Trent.

Lindsey was in shock. "Trent?" She got off her bike. He'd really come to Paris, after all.

"I wanted to surprise you," he said as he approached and kissed both her cheeks.

"Well, you did." It was an understatement. She put down the kickstand of her bike.

"Your assistant said you were staying here, and I thought it would be convenient," Trent said as J.P. began removing his bags from the car.

"Wow, how great," Lindsey said.

"You look beautiful. Come, let's have a drink." Trent took Lindsey's arm and led her to the door.

"Great," she said, completely caught off guard by the whole situation. Wait, what about Jack? She turned back to see him helping J.P. with Trent's bags. He looked at her and shrugged. She shrugged back then followed Trent inside. She didn't know what else to do.

Jack watched Lindsey leave on the arm

of the handsome, obviously wealthy American.

Jack had shared a magical afternoon with her. Finally, he'd gotten the chance to tell her how much he regretted the past. He knew now that she regretted it, too. For just a couple of hours, he'd felt like a young man again: fully alive, filled with hopes for the future.

But now, with the arrival of this intruder, maybe none of that would matter.

He turned to J.P. "Well, take care of his bags, I guess."

"And throw them in the street?" J.P. asked with a sly smile.

"Yeah," Jack said, and then quickly clarified. "No. I'm kidding. Bring them in."

Chapter Ten

The Smallest Space

ONCE INSIDE THE HOTEL, JACK made his way past Lindsey and Trent, went straight to the front desk, and took over for the clerk. Lindsey was surprised at Jack's urgency. She knew he was the owner of the hotel and all, but he looked like a man on a mission.

"Trent Greer? Correct?" Jack asked as he typed the name into the computer. Trent nodded. "I'm Jack Burrows, the owner. Welcome."

"Thank you," Trent said as he impatiently tapped his Black AMEX on the counter. He turned to Lindsey. "You two know each other?"

"We do." Lindsey nodded.

"Old friends," Jack said. "We go way back. Right, Linds?"

Lindsey nodded, but inwardly, she cringed. Jack hadn't shortened her name like that since the first week they met. She hated it and he knew it. He'd used it a few times after class when he'd found her talking with a couple of her male classmates. He'd never been possessive, but he liked to let others know that he was fond of her.

"I found your room and we're all set. I just need a credit card for incidentals," Jack said to Trent. Trent handed Jack his credit card. Jack ran it through the iPad attachment. "Sign here, and I'll take you to your room."

"That's okay, I think I can manage," Trent said as he signed the screen with his finger, then put his card back in his wallet.

"I insist," Jack said. "J.P. will follow with the bags. Lindsey, want to come with us?"

Lindsey nodded. She could tell Jack was up to something, but she didn't know what.

Jack led the two of them past the bar, through the courtyard, up the steps to the elevator, past the elevator, and to another set of stairs. They descended those stairs and walked through a narrow hallway. At the end of the hallway, Jack pulled back a door with a gilded grate and then found another dark wooden door behind it.

"Here we are," Jack said as he inserted the key and opened the room.

Jack pushed back the door and entered. Trent and Lindsey followed. The four-poster bed nearly touched the door, and the fire-place was two feet in front of the bed. Lindsey stood across from Trent as J.P. squeezed between them with the bags. "Excuse me," he said. Lindsey backed up against the wall.

"Well, this is cozy," Trent said. Cozy was an understatement. It was one of the tiniest hotel rooms Lindsey had ever seen, and she'd lived in New York City for the majority of her life, where tiny was the accepted norm.

Jack pulled the drapes back to reveal that the room was on the bottom floor and looked out into an alley.

"Where should I put these?" J.P. asked, holding up the luggage.

"The hallway?" Lindsey joked. "Can't you find him a better room?" she asked as Jack turned back toward them.

J.P. put the bags in a corner next to the window.

"Sorry. We're booked up. Valentine's Day," Jack said with a smile.

"That's not for a while yet," Lindsey said.

Jack shrugged. "You know Paris. Any excuse to celebrate love."

Lindsey shook her head. The holiday was a month away. Jack was up to no good. She knew it. She was about to say something to him, but J.P. squeezed back through the space between her and Trent.

Just as J.P. managed to open the door,

Trent stopped him. "Wait. This is for you." Trent held up fifty euros.

"Thank you, sir." J.P. grinned as he took the generous tip and left.

As Jack dusted off the mantel over the fireplace, Trent turned to Lindsey. "On the chance you're free tonight, I made a reservation for the three of us at St. Germaine."

"Oh man. I can't make it. I'm so sorry. I'm working the front desk tonight," Jack said as he turned and placed his hand on Trent's shoulder as if they were old pals.

"Actually, I meant Lindsey and her daughter," Trent said, shrugging Jack's hand off his shoulder.

"Oh. Duh. Of course. Sorry about that. Anything else I can help you with?" Jack asked.

"We're good. Thank you," Trent said, producing another fifty euros. Jack looked at the large bill. Lindsey watched as he contemplated taking it.

"You know what? You keep that. You're going to need it if you're going to St. Germaine, and if I were you, I would not order the fish." Jack scrunched his face and held up the key to the room.

Trent took the key. Jack stood still. Trent nodded to the door. "Great. Thank you very much. I think we're good now."

"Oh, right. I'll get going," Jack said.

Jack shimmied between the two of them to exit the room. "Excuse me," he said, then left.

When Jack was gone, Lindsey stepped back toward the window. They both took in the incredibly small space. "Wow," she said.

"Yeah," Trent replied, looking around.

"I'm not even sure this is a room," Lindsey said.

"I've been in smaller," Trent said as he ran his hand through the back of his hair.

"Really?"

"Never," Trent said as he shook his head. Lindsey laughed. Trent paused, then began, "I hope it's all right that I'm here. I just thought it was the perfect opportunity to show you our Paris office."

"You are persistent," Lindsey said. Trent's phone rang.

"Maybe after dinner we'll stop by the office," he said. The phone continued to ring. "Hold on one sec." Lindsey nodded. Trent picked up the phone. "Yep. I mean, it's not a great time, but you know." Trent looked at Lindsey and mouthed *I'm sorry.*

Lindsey understood. She and Trent shuffled side to side to allow her room to pass. She slowly slipped out into the hallway as Trent continued talking on the phone. He gestured with his hand that he'd see her later.

Lindsey walked back through the narrow hallway, up the stairs, and to the elevator, which she rode straight to her suite. Back in her room, she kicked off her boots and stretched out on the bed.

She'd always wanted Jack to return to her life so she could say, *It's too late*. Then her new boyfriend would appear, and make Jack insanely jealous. But what had just occurred was completely awkward. She and Jack had spent a lovely day together, Trent had shown up, Jack had gotten jealous, and now she was going to dinner with Trent for what seemed to be a work dinner—but she wasn't so sure.

She sighed and closed her eyes to take a quick nap.

Hugo and Kathryn had spent the entire afternoon combing through the locks on the Pont Neuf. They had started at the west end of the bridge and meticulously moved east, yet they had still come up empty-handed.

Kathryn could not remember the exact location of the lock, and now the bridge was covered with thousands of them. The entire thing was unrecognizable. When she and James had placed their lock on the iron fence, there was space all around theirs. Now there was no open space. It was no wonder the bridge could no longer handle the weight of the love locks.

Kathryn had wanted to give up the search, but Hugo had insisted they forge on. When darkness fell and they still hadn't found the lock, Hugo offered to take Kathryn to dinner at his favorite bistro. Feeling defeated, she had graciously accepted.

They entered into the small restaurant and were immediately greeted by the *maître'd*, who simply pointed toward the back. It was clear to Kathryn that Hugo had been there many times before.

"I'm sorry we couldn't find your lock," Hugo said as they approached their table. "Here, let me." He pulled her chair out for her.

"Thank you," Kathryn said as she sat and removed her coat. "It was good of you to indulge me. I don't know what I was thinking." Kathryn slouched in her chair.

"Well, you were thinking about love. Which does strange things to everyone. So, maybe I go back to the bridge and I take a flashlight and bolt cutters." He made a gesture with his hands simulating cutting the lock.

"If you do, you'll be arrested," she said.

"Wouldn't be the first time." Hugo smirked.

"Oh, dear," Kathryn said, chuckling.

After a moment, he took a deep breath. "It makes me happy to see you laugh," Hugo said.

Kathryn paused. "It's been a while." Since her husband's passing she hadn't allowed herself to enjoy much in life.

"Well, I know exactly what you need. How long has it been since you've had a decadent—" Hugo started, but Kathryn interrupted.

"Meal?" she interjected.

He shook his head. "Dessert," he finished.

She paused for a minute, it had definitely been a long time. Hugo raised his hand and called out to the *maître'd*, "*Un chocolate terrible*," he said, and then winked at her. "You're going to love this."

Kathryn smiled. She knew she would. Spending the day with Hugo had reminded her that life can't be planned—sometimes, you must go with its natural flow. And if that meant eating dessert for dinner, then she was happy to do it.

Lindsey and Trent sat at an intimate table at St. Germaine, one of the finest restaurants in Paris. Trent had taken the liberty to order their drinks, and Lindsey was toying with the napkin on her lap waiting for them to arrive.

"I'm sorry Alexa couldn't join us," Trent said.

"She didn't want to intrude. And she's busy falling in love with someone she's known for two days," Lindsey explained.

When Lindsey had woken from her nap that afternoon, she'd found a text of a photo of Alexa and J.P. outside the pyramid at the Louvre that said, "Don't worry about us. J.P. is taking good care of me, and we're going to dinner. I'll see you back at the hotel tonight." When Lindsey read the text, she thought about responding and telling Alexa that she had to come to dinner with her and Trent, but then she'd thought better. Things were already awkward enough. The last thing she needed was her daughter to be on her pseudo-date with her.

"Well, who hasn't fallen in love quickly, right?" Trent asked. Lindsey smiled. The waiter came and filled their glasses with champagne. Trent raised his glass and Lindsey followed suit.

"Are you trying to sweep me off my feet so you can get my magazine?" Lindsey asked as the bubbles fizzed.

"Please tell me it's working," Trent said.

"One foot's off the ground," Lindsey replied.

Trent clinked his glass against hers. "To the other foot."

"You are good," Lindsey said before she took a sip. After they both put their glasses down, there was a long, awkward moment of silence between them.

Finally, Trent said, "Lindsey, how about we don't talk business tonight."

"Oh, so this would be a..."

"Some would call it a date," Trent said, finishing her sentence.

"One of those," Lindsey said, not sure if she should act happy, surprised, or mad.

"Or not," Trent backpedaled.

Lindsey quickly recovered. "No. We could call it a date." Trent was gorgeous, and they were at one of the most romantic restaurants in the world. Plus, she had worn her lucky black dress that she'd packed at the last minute.

"Okay, good," Trent said.

"Sorry, I'm a little out of practice."

"Actually, I am, too," Trent said.

"Why do I find that hard to believe?"

Trent straightened his tie. Lindsey could tell he'd gotten this response from women before. "It's true," he said. "I work pretty much 24-7. But I am trying to change that." He paused, then added, "Starting thirty seconds ago."

Lindsey chuckled. She liked Trent. Despite the fact that he was a media mogul, he was humble and kind.

"How am I doing?" he asked.

"Pretty good," Lindsey said.

Just then a waiter arrived with caviar. Lindsey held up her plate as if to say, *yes please*, then turned back to Trent.

"Actually, you're doing very good," she said.

Trent grinned.

Back at the hotel, Jack was in his office. As night fell, work at the front desk settled into a lull, and he retreated to his desk for some alone time. He had come to contemplate the day he'd had with Lindsey. He was reminiscing about their time in school when he remembered the box.

The box was sturdy cardboard covered in red and gold. It was no ordinary container. It held photos and mementos. Every time Jack had moved offices, he had taken it with him. When he'd opened the hotel, he'd placed it at the back of a shelf and never looked at it again.

Now, ten years later, he carefully peeled off the top and found a stack of old photos of himself and Lindsey. He flipped through them. Each was a different memory of a time and a place. When he got to a black-and-white photo, he paused. It was the day he'd finally said *I love you*. He distinctly remembered how nervous he had been about telling her his true feelings. They were on a bike ride and had stopped on one of the bridges over the Seine. Lindsey had insisted he hold the camera away from them and snap a photo of the two of them together. Afterward, he'd turned to her and said the three words. She didn't even hesitate to say *I love you* back. That's when he knew she was special.

After a few minutes, Jack put the photos down and pulled out a rolled-up piece of paper. He unfolded it to find it was the sketch the artist had done of the two of them. It was old, but it hadn't faded. The same Eiffel Tower background that was in the sketch Lindsey and Alexa had done together was in theirs.

There was a small scratch at the door. "Yoo-hoo," a woman's voice said.

Jack looked up to find it was Nicole. "You're always working," she said as she walked down the two stairs into his office and placed her purse on the chair across from his desk.

"Oh, really? I always feel like I'm not working enough," he said. Nicole approached him, placed her hands on his cheeks, and pulled him in for a kiss.

When she backed away, she looked down to see the sketch. "I see she's more than just a hotel guest."

"This? Oh, come on. It was a lifetime ago," Jack said.

Nicole studied the painting. "You look happy."

"Well, everyone looks happy in sketches."

"Yeah, but not everyone digs up old pictures," she said.

Jack shook his head and tried to cover. "Maybe seeing her here has stirred up old memories. But I told you, it was a lifetime ago." That was the truth. He had no clue if the future held anything for them.

"When is she leaving?"

"A couple days." He knew that would make Nicole happy, but he wasn't sure how he felt about it.

Nicole gave him a coy look. "Is it possible she could leave sooner?"

Jack laughed. "Come on. Her life is in New York."

"That's good, because I'm going to Milan next weekend, and I want you to come with me," Nicole said.

Jack paused. A weekend away together was a step in the serious direction, and he'd only known Nicole for a few weeks. "Milan. Wow. I wish I could, but the hotel. I can't."

"Of course you can. It's your hotel."

Jack racked his brain for another excuse, but before he had to give one, he was literally saved by the bell of the front desk. "Coming!" Jack yelled out.

He took Nicole's hand and kissed it. "I'm sorry. Work calls," he said, then walked away, leaving Nicole alone.

Jack checked a woman in a red coat into the hotel. "You're all set," he said as he handed her the keys. "Enjoy your stay."

The woman followed the night bellhop toward the elevator. Jack turned to head back to Nicole and his office, when Lindsey and Trent entered.

Lindsey was so caught up in her conversation with Trent that she didn't even notice Jack until his cheerful voice boomed down the entranceway.

"Hey," he said. "How was St. Germaine?"

"Well, you were right. We shouldn't have ordered the fish," Trent said.

Jack pointed at Trent as if they were old buddies. "I told you."

Lindsey was about to add her two cents to the conversation and tell Jack about the amazing caviar they'd had when she was distracted by a cold breeze. The door had opened behind her. Jack took a step back.

Alexa and J.P. were returning to the hotel after a day around the city. Happy to see them, Lindsey tapped Trent on the shoulder.

"Trent, this is my daughter," Lindsey said, gesturing to Alexa.

"Alexa, so nice to meet you." Trent extended his hand to her.

She eyed him up and down. "You, too." Lindsey knew she was sizing him up, figuring out if he was good enough for her mother.

"And you've already met J.P.," Lindsey said in an effort to distract Alexa.

"Thank you again for that generous tip, sir," J.P. said. Trent nodded in a gesture of *you're welcome.*

"So, what have you two been up to tonight?" Lindsey asked. She loved hearing about the city through Alexa's eyes.

"We had so much fun," Alexa said.

"We had bread and cheese," J.P. said.

"And we walked along the Seine," Alexa added, completing his sentence.

"Don't forget the rock," J.P. said.

Alexa reached into her pocket. "We found a rock that's shaped like a heart," she said and held it up for everyone to see.

"It's good luck," J.P. added.

Lindsey couldn't help but smile at how effusive they were. "What'd you guys do?" Alexa asked her.

"We had an amazing dinner. And an amazing dessert. And then Trent showed me his offices here. Which are..."

"Amazing," Trent finished.

Just then, Nicole emerged from Jack's office. Jack stepped forward, inserting himself into the conversation.

"Oh, hey, guys. Here is my girlfriend, Nicole. Who is so... amazing," Jack said with a nod and a smile to Lindsey.

Lindsey gritted her teeth. The awkwardness had begun once again, but before things could get worse, Hugo and Kathryn entered the lobby. Lindsey's mood lifted immediately. *They're together.*

"Hello," Hugo said in his boisterous voice. "It's a party in the lobby. I love gatherings in small spaces." They walked toward the group.

"Trent, this is Kathryn Daltry," Lindsey said.

"Yes, the exquisite Kathryn Daltry," Hugo said, holding her chin up high with his left fingertips.

"Hugo, you're too kind," Kathryn objected.

"Well, no one's ever accused me of that before," Hugo said.

Lindsey pointed her finger at him. "Agreed." Everyone laughed. Lindsey turned to Trent for a proper introduction to Hugo. "And this is Hugo Blanchett, the artist."

"I'm more than that. But that'll do for now," Hugo said as he extended his hand to Trent.

Trent shook Hugo's hand. "Pleasure to meet you. Trent Greer."

"*Bonjour*, Mr. Greer," Hugo said.

Lindsey turned to Trent. "Hugo is Alexa's painting teacher."

Alexa turned around and added, "Yours, too."

Trent looked at Lindsey with a surprised look on his face. "I didn't know you painted."

Lindsey demurred. She never told people in her professional life that she was an artist herself before she started *POV,* and she hadn't had any intention of telling Trent.

"Well, it's sad to say, she's given it up," Hugo said.

Lindsey looked away, embarrassed by the attention. She didn't want to talk about the fact that she gave up painting because it was attached to far more. She looked at Kathryn with a quiet desperation.

"You're not going to believe what we did tonight. Hugo took me to Pont Neuf. We searched for hours for my lock," Kathryn said. Lindsey sighed relief. Bullet dodged.

Alexa's eyes widened. "You have a lock on the bridge?"

"Yes. I thought I might find it before the city cuts them off," Kathryn said.

"Cuts them off?" Alexa asked. It was clear this was the first time she had heard this news. "They can't cut them off. The love locks are a part of Paris. They're a part of people's history."

"Yes, well, they have their reasons, I suppose," Kathryn said, though she sounded thoroughly unconvinced.

"That's awful." Alexa looked back at Jack, who nodded in agreement. She turned to her mom for reassurance, but Lindsey couldn't give it to her. She didn't believe in the bridge or love or happily ever after.

"It's just a bridge, sweetie," Lindsey said.

"Yeah, but all those promises."

"I'll admit, I'm a bit sentimental about it, too," Kathryn said.

"You know what we should all do? Go to the bar," Hugo interrupted. "I'm going to buy drinks for everyone," he said as he walked through the group and headed toward the bar. "Put it on my tab."

"Hugo, you don't have a tab," Jack said.

Everyone laughed and headed to the bar. For the next hour, they all sipped their drinks and talked about their favorite sights in Paris, but no one mentioned the bridge again.

After drinks, everyone said goodbye and goodnight. Lindsey and Alexa headed upstairs to their room where Lindsey was hit with a full barrage of questions. Alexa wanted to know how dinner with Trent had gone, how Lindsey felt about Jack, and about the future of *POV*.

"Did you decide?" Alexa asked as they approached their door.

"About what?" Lindsey asked.

"The magazine," Alexa said.

Lindsey paused with a smile, then answered, "Actually, we didn't even talk about it."

"So it was a date?" Alexa asked curiously.

Lindsey could say nothing except, "Kind of."

"Mom, but what about Jack?" she asked.

"What about him?" Lindsey laughed. Jack had a girlfriend—or something. She and Jack had a past, and they had definitely shared a moment, but that was it. Right?

"So... I get to call Dad and tell him you're not just seeing somebody, but you're seeing two somebodies." Alexa giggled.

"I am not." Lindsey pointed her finger at Alexa as if she were a little girl about to do the thing she'd been warned not to do. "And don't you dare call your dad."

Alexa laughed. "Oh, I'm gonna."

Lindsey playfully spanked Alexa and she ran ahead. Lindsey held back and thought about what Alexa had said. She clearly wasn't seeing two people, but could she be? Or would she have to make a choice? And if so, who would she choose? Jack or Trent?

Chapter Eleven

Pennies for Thoughts

AS THE SUN ROSE OVER Paris, Lindsey lay
in bed thinking about Jack and Trent.
She weighed the pros and cons of both. She
and Jack had history. Their relationship was
familiar and easy, yet there was that whole
heartbreak thing that happened twenty years
ago. She and Trent were new and exciting.
He was ambitious and direct. He knew what
he wanted and didn't hesitate to go after it.

Jack owned the hotel and had confessed
that his life was the business. He would never come to New York. It would be the same
thing all over again. Trent, on the other hand,
traveled everywhere, yet was based in New
York. He also wanted to buy her magazine.
He would certainly not be leaving anytime
soon.

Thoughts of each ran through her head.
The winter sun became brighter. By the time

it had fully illuminated her room, Alexa came bounding in.

"Good. You're awake. I couldn't sleep in," Alexa said. "I'm so excited about Hugo's show tonight."

"Me too. I couldn't sleep any longer, either," Lindsey lied. While she was certainly eager to see the show, it was the thoughts of Jack and Trent that had woken her so early.

"Remember when we used to watch the sun rise in Queens?" Alexa asked as she sat on the bed and gazed out the window.

"Those were some of my favorite mornings."

Alexa laid back on the pillow next to Lindsey's. "Mine, too," she said. "I'm going to miss you, Mom."

"I'll miss you, too," Lindsey replied. "But you are happy to be here, right?" Lindsey asked out of concern. After all, she was still a mother.

"Oh my gosh. Yes. Absolutely! I guess a part of me wishes you were going to be here, too, painting," Alexa said.

"My time has passed. I have the magazine back in New York, and that's where my life is. But you get to live this adventure, and I want you to enjoy every moment," Lindsey told her.

"Don't worry. I will," Alexa said. "And

even if things don't continue with J.P., Paris will still be amazing."

"That's good," Lindsey said, happy to hear that Alexa wasn't basing her entire Paris experience on a boy.

"Though, I really hope things work out with us." Alexa turned to her with a big grin.

"I hope they do, too," Lindsey said, and she meant it. Love was beautiful when it worked. She'd just never experienced it, but that didn't mean she couldn't hope for it for her daughter.

"All right. Well, I'm going to get ready for breakfast. Aren't we meeting Trent downstairs in twenty minutes?" Alexa asked.

Lindsey nodded. She had completely forgotten that she'd agreed to breakfast with Trent since Alexa hadn't been able to make dinner the night before. "We are," she said. "I'm hopping in the shower now."

Alexa got out of Lindsey's bed and headed to her room, but before she disappeared, she turned back. "Wear something cute. You never know what could happen."

Lindsey picked up her pillow and playfully threw it at Alexa. "Go get ready," she said.

"Okay," Alexa said. "I'm just saying. Trent is pretty hot for an old dude." Lindsey picked up the other pillow and held it above her head as a playful threat. "Fine. Fine.

I'll see you downstairs," Alexa said as she bounced off into the other room.

Lindsey got out of bed and opened the giant armoire. She pulled out a gray V-neck cashmere sweater and a pair of skinny jeans and laid them on her bed. The outfit looked put together but not as if she was trying too hard. It's perfect, Lindsey thought as she headed to the shower to get ready for the day.

Trent, ever the businessman, wore a suit to breakfast. Alexa had on an off-the-shoulder cable-knit sweater that Lindsey watched J.P. admire as he poured coffee for the three of them.

Trent was leading the conversation. "Alexa," he said, "my company is sponsoring a concert series at Le Zenith next weekend. And I thought I would leave two tickets for you and J.P. at will call." J.P. stopped pouring the coffee. Lindsey noticed. "If your mom's okay with that," Trent added.

"Yes, of course," Lindsey said.

"Thank you," Alexa said.

"That's so nice," Lindsey responded. Not only was Trent charming with her, but with Alexa, as well.

J.P. finished pouring the coffee, and Trent put his napkin on the table. "I'm so sorry to cut this breakfast short, but I have to run," he said, then turned to Lindsey. "Are you sure you won't come with me?"

Trent had wanted her to tag along with him that morning to several meetings at his magazine so she could see what operations were like in his companies. While Lindsey was slightly intrigued, her trip to Paris was not supposed to be about business.

"Thanks, but we're helping Hugo set up for his show," Lindsey said. Out of the corner of her eye, she saw Jack peek his head around the corner.

"Right, right. What time is that?" Trent asked. Hugo had told him about it over drinks the night before, but Lindsey hadn't seen him add it to his calendar.

"4:00 p.m.," Lindsey said.

"The Archive?" Trent asked.

Lindsey nodded. "The Archive."

Trent looked at his phone. "I have a four o'clock editors' meeting, but I'll meet you there." His phone began ringing.

"Sounds like a plan," Lindsey said. Jack looked around the wall again. Lindsey wondered what he wanted.

"Perfect." Trent grabbed his briefcase, answered the call, and walked away.

Once Trent was out of sight, Jack approached their table with a brown paper bag. He set it in front of Lindsey and sat in Trent's empty seat.

"Hey, would you mind taking these to Hugo for me?" he asked.

"What is it?" Lindsey asked.

"Umm, they're croissants," Jack said. "I lost a bet." He picked up Trent's dirty plate, got up, and walked away.

Lindsey looked at Alexa. *What was that all about?* Alexa shrugged her shoulders. It was apparent neither had a clue.

Trent had already signed the meal to his room, so when they were finished, they gathered their belongings and headed outside. They made the twenty-minute walk through the city to Hugo's studio.

Hugo was busy crating his art to be moved to the gallery when Lindsey and Alexa entered. Lindsey came in holding up the bag Jack had given her.

"Ah, croissants," Hugo said as they entered.

"From Jack." Lindsey handed the bag to Hugo. She and Alexa followed him into the center of the studio.

"A man of honor," Hugo said, taking the bag.

"I'm not even going to ask what the bet was," Lindsey said.

"That's a good choice," Hugo replied.

Lindsey took a look around the studio. Almost every painting had been crated and carried away. "Hey, where is everything?" she asked.

"Oh, it went to the gallery. They're coming for the last load," Hugo explained.

"I thought we were going to help," Lindsey said as Alexa walked alongside her.

"Well, you are," Hugo said as he led them to the only canvas left uncrated. Lindsey and Alexa took it in. Both of their eyes opened wide.

It was Lindsey's unfinished love locks bridge painting.

"What is this?" Lindsey asked.

"You see, this could be your best work," Hugo said.

"Hugo," Lindsey cried. She wasn't ready to paint. Especially not a painting that was so connected to her past. "I don't know about this."

"The first step back is you take the brush." Hugo pulled a brush from his pocket.

"No. Alexa can finish it," Lindsey said and backed away. She had no interest in completing that painting. The colors were still off, and it had been too long since she'd last painted.

"Alexa has her own life to paint," Hugo said. "You need to finish yours."

Hugo had a point, but Lindsey was still hesitant. "What if I can't?"

Hugo sighed. "Of course you can. Now, while you are here, allow yourself to be the artist."

Lindsey looked at him, frightened. She shook her head.

"Take the brush," he said as he placed it in her hand and nodded that she could do it. "And Alexa and I will be putting together the gallery for a brilliant show." Hugo led Alexa away from the painting, leaving Lindsey alone.

As Lindsey stood in front of the canvas, she could hear Hugo educating Alexa about the gallery. "Now, the most important thing about hanging art is the light," Hugo explained. "You can make a bad painting look like a masterpiece." Lindsey looked over as he grabbed his coat and reached down to a turntable. He put on some classical music and looked back at Lindsey. She took off her own coat and rolled up her sleeves. With a nod and a smile to Lindsey, Hugo turned around and led Alexa out of the building.

The music wafted through the room and Lindsey stared at her painting. She didn't know where to begin, but then she remembered Hugo had always said to start with the color. She remembered the orange sunset she'd always tried to replicate and began mixing paints. She spent an hour combining paints, and for the first time, it looked as if she was close to getting the correct color.

Lindsey smiled and began to paint. Stroke after stroke, her rhythm returned to her and she became engrossed in her art. Maybe she hadn't lost everything.

She didn't know if she would finish the piece, and she didn't care. It felt good to be painting again, as if a part of her past had returned and woken her to the present.

For the next three hours, she continued to paint until her arms began cramping from the repetitive movements.

The painting was three-quarters of the way done. She thought about skipping Hugo's show to finish it but decided that the painting had sat unfinished for twenty years—what was another day?

Chapter Twelve

For the Love of Art

T HE ENTRANCE TO THE ARCHIVE Gallery
was lined with giant Roman statues. A
red carpet led Alexa, J.P., Lindsey, and Kathryn straight into the great room. The four
were dressed for the occasion.

Lindsey wore a black jumpsuit, and
Alexa was in black pants and a black lace
top. She and J.P. entered holding hands. The
great room was a wide-open space. The gallery was three floors, and the top two looked
down into the main area. People milled
about, sipping champagne and wine.

Hugo entertained a wealthy couple who
had stopped to admire one of his paintings.
"Art, like love, has no cure. If it's true, it will
stay with you," Hugo said with confidence.

The salt-and pepper-haired man smiled
and nodded. "Are you trying to sell us a
painting, Hugo?"

"Of course," Hugo charmed. The three

chuckled. "But I mean every word." Hugo walked off. The man straightened his tie and turned to his wife.

"This would look good in the study," he said. His wife nodded.

"It would," she said. "But let's keep looking around." The couple traversed through the crowd and passed by J.P. and Alexa, who were making their way through the gallery.

J.P., who had dressed in a dark gray tailored shirt and black slacks, could not let go of Alexa's hand. "One day, you'll be hanging your work here," he said, turning to Alexa.

"Maybe. One day," Alexa said. "But right now, let's go back to that conversation we were just having."

"About us?" J.P. asked.

Alexa nodded. "So, when my semester's over, you can come to New York."

"I can apply to grad school," J.P. added without missing a beat.

"We can have the whole summer together. I'll show you all the sights. Starting with the Statue of Liberty, which is actually..."

"French," J.P. said, finally getting a word in. Alexa was going a mile a minute.

They both laughed as they passed a painting of a man blurring his hands through the air. While they continued planning their future, Kathryn and Lindsey analyzed a painting of crashing waves at the sea.

"It makes you feel like you're there," Kathryn said.

Lindsey nodded. "Hugo does have a way with nature."

"He really is quite talented."

Lindsey she spotted Hugo approaching. "Yes, he is."

"Kathryn," Hugo said in his delightful French accent. "You made it."

"Well, I realized it was something I just did not want to miss," Kathryn said.

"I'm so glad you came." Hugo linked his fingers in hers. "Come, I show you something." Lindsey trailed behind as Hugo led Kathryn through the crowds to a portrait at the far end of the room.

Kathryn stared at the painting of her, speechless. "Oh, wow," she finally said. Lindsey smiled. She was glad she had introduced the two of them. Hugo had captured Kathryn's emotions perfectly. Not only that, he had also added an antique lock in her hands. Lindsey looked at Kathryn whose eyes were welling up at the image.

"Did I make you cry?" Hugo asked, then placed his hand on her shoulder.

She shook her head and a smile crept across her face. "You made me look, so... so full of life," she managed to say. The tears were tears of joy.

Hugo gestured to her, then the painting. "Well, I paint what I see."

"It's just that I've felt so sad," Kathryn said, continuing to take in the painting. "And this makes it look like there's hope."

"Look, you can see both," he said, pointing to the eyes of the painting. "Life and love. It's complicated. That's what makes them great."

Kathryn sighed. "Thank you, Hugo."

"My pleasure, madame." He placed his arm around the small of her back, and they looked into each other's eyes. There was a moment of hesitation and then they kissed. Slowly at first, then a bit more passionately.

As they were locked in the embrace, several other patrons gathered to admire the portrait of Kathryn. Lindsey made her way to an abstract painting that had caught her eye in another section of the gallery.

She had always been more of a realist, but she appreciated the abstract, especially when it had a deeper meaning. Her eyes moved from corner to corner of the canvas, taking it all in. She was fully immersed in the painting when Jack approached.

"Oh yeah, there we go," Jack started. "I see it. It's a hamburger and a spatula. No, wait a minute. That's a grilled cheese and a spatula."

Lindsey shook her head. "You must be

hungry." She then went on to explain, "It's supposed to be two people in love. At least, that's what Hugo says."

Jack looked at the painting. "Oh, yeah, I see it now."

Lindsey turned to him. "Really?"

Jack smiled. "No," he said.

Lindsey laughed, then realized she hadn't expected to see Jack that evening. "I didn't know you were coming."

"Uh, Hugo invited me," he said in a way that made it seem he was lying. Lindsey wondered if he had decided to attend after he'd overheard her and Trent making plans to go together.

She turned away from the painting and went to the railing behind them. Jack followed. They were on the second floor of the gallery and looked out over the main gallery area. Lindsey leaned against the white wrought-iron rail.

They looked out at the crowds below. "Where's Nicole?" Lindsey asked, wondering if she would pop up behind them at any moment.

"Hugo said there wasn't enough room for a plus-one," he said.

They both looked at the crowd below. Clearly, there was plenty of room, but Hugo had been meddling again. "Hmmm, he never gives up," Lindsey said.

"There's something to be said about that," Jack said, then asked, "Where's your plus-one?"

"He had business. He'll be here later," Lindsey explained.

"Great," Jack said, but Lindsey could sense his lack of enthusiasm.

"So... publishing," Jack said in a way that made it seem as if he was fishing for information.

"Yep. Publishing," Lindsey said.

"Let me guess how you guys met. You met at a quaint little bookshop in Soho. You walked in, and your eyes met. You both reached for the same Renoir book..."

"Close," Lindsey said. "An editor's convention with five hundred people."

"Oh, hot," Jack said sarcastically. Lindsey nodded. "Be still my beating heart," he said, placing his right hand over his chest.

"How did you and Nicole meet?" Lindsey asked. If Jack could ask about Trent, then she could ask about Nicole.

"Sort of a similar romantic story. We were both in the waiting area of a dental office," Jack explained.

"Hmmm," Lindsey muttered. "Sexy." She didn't have much else to say. There was a moment of silence between them, then Jack broke it.

"Do you remember how we met?" he asked.

"Art history class," Lindsey said without a doubt. She still remembered him bringing her the Kleenex and Benadryl after.

"No, actually, we met before that," Jack explained.

Lindsey was shocked. "Really?"

"Yeah. You were painting on the Pont des Arts bridge. I pedaled past you. You smiled and waved." Jack mimicked how she waved.

"I don't remember that," Lindsey said in awe.

"Yeah. That's the whole reason I enrolled in the art history class," he told her nonchalantly. Lindsey was taken aback. This entire time, she thought he had just been a nice guy who helped her after her allergy attack, but it turned out he was a nice guy with an agenda to meet a girl. It was the kind of story of fairy tales. Guy sees girl, falls in love, makes plans to meet her, then makes it seem like chance that they ended up together.

"How come you never told me that?" Lindsey asked.

She waited for an explanation, but all he said was, "Well, I am now."

Lindsey stood silently, looking into Jack's eyes. She had always thought she knew everything about Jack. That she had him completely figured out, but now he had thrown a curveball into the story she had always told herself. Before she had a chance to ask Jack more questions, Alexa came bouncing down the spiral staircase from the floor above. J.P. was in tow.

"Mom," she said, interrupting Lindsey's train of thought, "J.P.'s coming to New York for summer break."

"Wow," Lindsey said, then turned to share a knowing look with Jack.

"I know, right?" Alexa was overjoyed. "And..."

"There's more?" Lindsey asked as she attempted to hide her panic by keeping a straight face.

"Look what he gave me," Alexa said as she began to dig through her purse.

Lindsey and Jack stood with eyes wide open, muttering to each other, "Don't be a ring. Don't be a ring."

Alexa finally pulled the gift from her purse.

"A lock," Lindsey said, relieved.

Alexa looked at J.P., then the lock. "We're putting it on the bridge. And I don't care if they cut it off or they melt it down, it's ours." She held the lock to her heart and looked into J.P.'s eyes.

Lindsey and Jack shared a smile at the announcement. They too had been that naive and in love once.

Before anyone could say any more, glasses began to clink in an effort to garner the attention of everyone in the gallery. They looked down and saw Hugo standing in the middle of the room.

"Hello," he said. "Madames and monsieurs." The crowd quieted and turned its attention to him. "Thank you. Thank you all for joining me here today, my friends, my colleagues." Hugo looked up and out at everyone who was in attendance. "We have shared many moments together. Some good, some not so good. But as the great John W. Gardner said, 'Life is the art of drawing without an eraser.'"

Lindsey and Jack shared a knowing look at the iteration of the quote.

"Many of you have asked what defines my art," Hugo continued. "What a question I cannot answer. Art is not what you see, but what you make others see," he said as he looked up at J.P. and Alexa, who were still standing on the open staircase. "So, eat, drink, enjoy the work, and if you see something you can't live without—don't," he finished as he threw his hands into the air for emphasis. The crowd applauded with laughter.

As they dispersed, Jack turned to Lindsey. "You see anything you can't live without?" he asked. There was a long pause.

Lindsey was about to respond when her phone rang. It was Trent. She smiled and excused herself as she answered the call and walked away.

Jack watched as she made her way to another part of the balcony. He stood for a moment and wondered if he should wait for her, but decided to wander away on his own. Jack walked down the stairs where he found Kathryn staring at a seascape.

When she saw him, she turned with a smile. He approached and sat on a stool in front of her.

"Hey, Kathryn," he said as he glanced up at Lindsey.

"Hey," she replied, then went on. "Are you going to tell her?"

"What?" Jack asked, playing dumb.

"That you're still in love with her," Kathryn said. "I couldn't help but notice."

Though she was correct in her observation Jack was still debating what to do with Lindsey. Their history was rife with heartache and mistakes. He worried that if he confessed his love for her, he would just make things worse.

Jack took a deep breath and gazed up at Lindsey, who was still pacing on the phone. She hadn't once looked back to see where he had gone. Perhaps things were better this way.

"No," he decided. "I'm not going to tell her."

Kathryn looked at him, concerned. "Jack, we rarely get a second chance."

"Her life is there. My life is here. What's the point? She's leaving," Jack said. He didn't want to repeat the past.

"So, you're just going to bury your feelings?" Kathryn pried.

"Yeah. It's been working for me so far," he explained.

"Has it?" Kathryn asked. "Because in all the years I've stayed at your hotel, you've been alone. Or with a different girl that you don't seem to care all that much about."

Jack hung his head. Kathryn was right. He had spent the past twenty years living a solitary bachelor life. Though he wasn't completely happy with his choices, he didn't know how to change them. He felt stuck. He was about to ask Kathryn for advice when Hugo approached.

"Kathryn, someone wants to buy your portrait," Hugo said.

Kathryn turned from Jack to Hugo. "Oh dear, have they had too much champagne?"

"Well, I told them it's not for sale, but they want to meet you anyway," Hugo said, clasping his hands around hers.

"Okay," Kathryn said as she allowed Hugo to lead her away. She looked back at

Jack once more, who gave her a half smile. Jack stood up and stared at the landscape of the sea. It was not lost on him that part of the problem with his relationship with Lindsey was that there was an entire ocean between them.

While he was taking in the painting, Lindsey walked down the stairs with two flutes of champagne in hand. She approached Jack.

"Well, looks like my plus-one just turned into a minus-one," she said, then handed him one of the glasses.

Jack took the champagne then held it up. "Here's to the plusses and the minuses," he said as he clinked his drink with hers. They looked into each other's eyes and took a sip.

For the next half hour, they wandered the gallery together, Lindsey explaining each painting and Jack asking a million questions. It was as if they were back in college again, and she was helping him study for their art history exam. When they had exhausted all their options, they decided to walk back to the hotel together.

Lindsey and Jack parted ways with Alexa and J.P., planning to see them back at the hotel in an hour. "Hugo must be happy," Lindsey said to Jack.

"He was sold out. I can't even do that in

my hotel," Jack said, leading Lindsey out of the gallery and into the city streets.

They crossed the street and headed toward the river. "You were sold out when Trent checked in," Lindsey stated.

Jack nodded. "Right, about that."

Lindsey playfully elbowed him. "You put him in that room on purpose, didn't you?"

"What? No. I would never," Jack said guiltily.

"Yes, you did." Lindsey laughed.

"All right. All right. I'm sorry."

"No you're not," Lindsey joked.

"You know that room really isn't even that small," Jack explained.

"It was a closet," Lindsey bantered back.

"I've seen rooms way smaller than that." Granted, that was when he was backpacking through Europe on a tight budget, but still, he had seen them.

"Seriously?"

"Yeah. You remember my dorm room," he said remembering how incredibly small it was. Lindsey had visited it exactly twice. The first time was to see where he lived, and the second was to confirm that she had no intention of spending the night there. Ever. The place was not meant for two people, she had said. "That room was bad."

"Remember that poster you had of the dogs playing poker?" Lindsey asked.

"I still have it," Jack said. "I loved that poster. That little bulldog. He's holding the pocket ace in his little hand."

"Paw," Lindsey corrected.

"Foot," Jack replied. Lindsey looked at him. "Whatever. That dog can handle his cards." Lindsey laughed.

They continued walking along the river, talking and reminiscing. They became so wrapped up in their conversation that they didn't notice they were at the foot of the Pont Neuf bridge until Jack looked up.

"Oh, boy. Here we go," Jack said as they approached.

"What?" Lindsey asked.

Jack pointed down the bridge. In the moonlight, the locks glistened along its railings. "You, me, locks, and a bridge," Jack said as they started walking across the bridge. "I feel like we've done this before."

Lindsey took it all in. "Too many locks, not enough keys," she said softly.

"You know, I didn't drop that lock on purpose that day," Jack said. He finally had the courage to tell her the truth. "I was scared."

"I know," Lindsey said. They looked at each other and their gazes held.

Jack sighed. "I guess I could've jumped on a plane to New York. Made some grand romantic gesture." Jack shook his head, not at

Lindsey, but at his terrible mistake. "I waited too long. We had our moment, and I let it slip away."

Lindsey shook her head. "We both let it slip away."

Jack wasn't buying it. "I could've gotten a job at a hotel in New York."

"I could've come back here, too," Lindsey added.

"So, what stopped us?" Jack asked. They both had the option to pursue the other, but no one had taken the step forward.

Lindsey's eyes welled with tears. "Maybe that's all we were supposed to be," she said. "Young love."

"Maybe we were supposed to be more, and we just got distracted," Jack said, hope still stirring in his chest. He'd always wondered what they could've been.

"Jack, let's just leave it at what it was," Lindsey said sadly.

His hope evaporated. He wanted to say more, but he respected her wishes and dropped the subject.

They finished the rest of their walk to the hotel in silence.

When they got back to the large wooden doors, Jack opened them for her. "Thank you for a nice evening," she said as she took off her jacket. "I guess we should call it a night."

But Jack didn't want the night to end.

In the silence, Jack had thought of a million things to say to Lindsey, but now, he was speechless. All he could say was...

"You wouldn't happen to be hungry by any chance, would you?" he asked.

"Starving," she said.

"Follow me," Jack said, relieved at her response.

"You still throw pasta on the ceiling?" he asked as they walked toward the dining area.

"Of course," she said. "You?"

"It's the only way to know if it's done." Jack led her into the dining room and into the small busboy area that held wine and a small refrigerator.

"Some things never change."

"Change is good, right?" He handed her two wineglasses. Lindsey had always been a little pessimistic, and Jack had always taken it upon himself to present her a more optimistic view.

"Eh," Lindsey said with a twist of her head.

"That doesn't really sound like a ringing endorsement," Jack said as he opened the small fridge and started to remove leftover containers of food.

Lindsey sighed. "I guess I'm scared."

"Of what?" Jack asked as he stacked the food on the counter.

"Of losing control of everything," she

said. "You know. I'm saying goodbye to Alexa. If I say goodbye to my business, what do I have left?"

"Yourself," Jack said. "You have yourself left." Jack pulled some more food out and placed it on a tray.

"So if someone wanted to buy your hotel, you'd sell it?" she asked.

Jack thought about it for a second. The hotel was his life, but...

"Well, that would depend on how much they were offering," Jack said as he grabbed a bottle of wine and the tray of food and walked back into the dining area. Lindsey followed him to a large table set in front of a fireplace. "You know, I could always start a new hotel," he explained.

"Oh, so much for that commitment," Lindsey said as he set down their dinner.

"Come on, Lindsey. These are things. Things can be replaced. People can't." Jack knew this all too well. He had been trying to replace Lindsey for years, but he could never find anyone quite like her.

"But what if that thing is who you are?" Lindsey still wasn't buying his response.

"It's *not* who you are," he said as he placed his coat on the back of his chair and sat down.

Lindsey did the same, then said, "You hardly know me anymore, Jack."

"Um, I think I do," he said and started to parcel the meats and cheeses out onto plates. "You're that girl on the bridge with her paint box and big dreams." He set down a piece of bread and looked at her.

"Yeah, well, all that's left of that dream is a magazine about other people's art," Lindsey said.

"It sounds like you got to learn to let go," Jack said. "If you can't let go, you'll never get to the other side. Trust me, I should know."

Jack had never made it to the other side, because Lindsey had always been on his mind. He handed her a plate of food and poured a glass of wine. They began to eat.

"You're right," she said. "I do have to let go, I just don't know how yet."

Jack tore off a piece of bread. "You'll figure it out. I know you will."

"Thanks," Lindsey said. "This is nice."

"Anytime." He poured more wine.

They continued to enjoy their meal, talking like they used to on their picnics. Nothing special. Nothing profound. Just an ordinary moment. A moment that Jack would not soon forget.

Just as they were beginning to feel full, Trent entered the hotel.

"There you are," Trent said as he stood on the stair that led into the main dining area.

Startled, Lindsey dropped her napkin. She and Jack rose from their seats.

"How was your meeting?" she asked.

"It was good," Trent responded. "I'm sorry I missed the show. And I was hoping to take you to dinner." He looked at the empty plates on the table. "But I see that I'm a little late."

"Oh, yeah. This was kind of spur-of-the-moment," Lindsey said. Jack smiled at Trent because he knew it was far more. He watched as Trent looked at her without a word.

Jack interrupted the silence. "Listen, on the bright side, I moved you to another room."

Trent stepped down the stairs. "Oh good. Smaller, right?"

Jack laughed. "No. A suite. Compliments of the owner."

"I appreciate that. Thank you," Trent said. "Um, Jack, is the bar still open?"

"Absolutely," Jack said. "As soon as I put on an apron." He was in the hotel business, after all, and the customer's needs always came first.

Trent held his hand out for Lindsey to follow him.

At the bar, Trent ordered a rare bottle of Pinot Noir. As Jack returned from the cellar, Trent was saying, "We can turn *POV* into something bigger and better. Isn't that what you had in mind when you started it?"

Lindsey pulled the shorter layers of her blonde hair back from her face. "I'm pretty sure when I started, all I wanted was to pay the rent."

"Well, that won't be a problem anymore," Trent said.

"And my staff?" Lindsey asked. Jack opened the bottle of wine and set two glasses in front of them.

"I can take some of them on," Trent said.

"How about all of them?" Lindsey asked, all business.

"Do you have an office dog you want us to take on as well?" Trent joked.

"No, but there's a pigeon who lives on the window ledge," Lindsey said lightly.

"Hmmm, all right. Corner office for the pigeon, but that's as far as I go."

Jack poured a sample of the wine for Trent, who swirled it, sniffed it, then sipped it. "That's great," he said.

"Does anyone ever say no to you?" Lindsey asked.

"You actually still have not said yes," he said. "And, Lindsey, I get it. This magazine is your baby."

Lindsey nodded. "Yeah, well, babies grow up, right? They leave the nest and fly away. Maybe it's time for me to say goodbye."

Jack was shocked at her response but kept his reaction to himself. Maybe he still could influence Lindsey in more ways than he realized.

"Is that a yes?" Trent asked.

Lindsey took a deep breath. "That's a yes. I'm in."

Jack smiled. Good for her.

"Congratulations." Trent held out his hand. "I'm so thrilled. That's wonderful."

Lindsey was about to hug Trent when Jack interrupted. "Sorry, I couldn't help but overhear. Congratulations!" Jack placed their now full glasses in front of them.

"Thank you," Lindsey said.

Trent held up his wine to toast with Lindsey. They tapped their glasses together and took a sip. "I think we should go and celebrate," Trent said.

"Now?" Lindsey asked.

"Top of the Eiffel Tower. I made us a reservation on the chance you would say yes," Trent said.

"Once again, sorry to interrupt, but the Eiffel Tower is going to be closed," Jack interjected. He didn't want Lindsey to leave with Trent.

Trent shook his head. "Not tonight, it's not."

"You must have friends in high places," Jack said with a tinge of jealousy.

Trent nodded. "Thankfully, I do."

Jack looked to Lindsey to see what she was going to do next.

She turned to Trent. "You know, if you don't mind, I think I'll go for a walk. I've got a lot to think about."

Jack gave a sigh of relief, but hoped Lindsey hadn't noticed. He was happy she wasn't going to the most romantic spot in the city with Trent, but he was also bummed that she wasn't staying behind to continue her talk with him.

"That's probably a good idea. Sure," Trent said in an accommodating manner.

"Good night and good night," Lindsey said to Jack and Trent as she walked off to the front door, leaving them behind.

While Lindsey made her way across town, Hugo made his way to the hotel and called on Kathryn. It was late in the evening, but she came down to meet him in the lobby library area.

"I'm sorry to call at this hour," he said as he paced in front of a bookshelf.

"Is everything all right?" Kathryn asked, concerned.

"Well, I hope so," Hugo said as he handed a brass object to her.

Kathryn looked down and examined the metal piece. It was the lock inscribed *Kathryn and James*, and it had been cut.

"You found it," Kathryn said with tears in

her eyes. She sat down and took it in. She was overcome with emotion. "I never thought I'd see it again. Thank you." She looked up at Hugo, whose own eyes were filled with tears, as well.

After his show, Hugo had gone back to the bridge to find the lock. The painting was one thing, but this was another. He knew a painting could never replace the real thing, and he had to get it for her. Because art is what you can make others see. And that lock made Kathryn see that love was still alive.

He smiled. "You're welcome."

Lindsey walked into her bedroom to find Alexa lying on her belly, typing on her phone.

"You're up."

Alexa sat up in bed. "And I want details. Starting with the moment I saw you leave the gallery with Jack."

Lindsey untied her jacket. "Do I interrogate you when you come in late?" she asked, laughing at how their roles had changed.

"Are you kidding?" Alexa asked. "You're like a CSI investigator. So... ?"

Lindsey relented. "We walked, we talked, we ate. Trent showed up. And... I decided to sell the magazine." Lindsey put her jacket down on the chair and looked at Alexa. She wanted to see her reaction, because then she'd know if she'd made the right choice.

Alexa's eyes went wide. "What? Mom, are you sure?"

Lindsey shook her head, then sat on the bed next to Alexa. She felt unsure, but she knew it was the right choice. "I've been trying to keep everything the same. You. Our life. But things change. They grow up. And that's okay."

Alexa smiled, opened her arms wide, and wrapped them around her. They closed their eyes and held their heads close, the same way they had hugged for years. "I'm proud of you. It's going to be great. I know it."

They untangled their arms and looked at each other. "Thanks, sweetie," Lindsey said.

"Look at you," Alexa started. "A few days ago, you were in your lonely apartment, hiding art in your closet. And now you're in Paris with two men half in love with you."

Lindsey shook her head. "Ha ha. No one's in love with me. Not even half in love with me."

"Jack is," Alexa stated.

Lindsey paused and thought about it for a moment. Alexa might be right, but she wasn't ready for that truth. Selling her business was enough change for one night. "That's ridiculous," she said.

"Is it?" Alexa asked.

"You've been in Paris four days, and you're an expert on love?" Lindsey deflected.

"I'm an expert on you," Alexa said. There was no denying the truth in that fact. Alexa and she knew each other inside and out. Love was something they could never explain, only understand. Lindsey wrapped her arms around Alexa. As they hugged, she thought about their past, their present, and their future.

Everything around her could change, but their bond would always have a time and a place.

Chapter Thirteen

The Long Goodbye

LINDSEY WOKE THAT MORNING WITH the sinking feeling that everything was about to change.

With the sale of *POV*, she would have more free time and extra cash. She looked forward to the end of winter and the beginning of something new. Until then, however, she dreaded what was next.

The last day in Paris would be marked by goodbyes. She'd be saying goodbye to Alexa and heading back to New York where she would begin the transition of handing *POV* off to Trent Greer's publishing empire. She also knew she would have to say goodbye to Jack. The last time they'd said goodbye, they'd made promises that were never kept. Today, she planned to leave with a goodbye and *I'll see you later*. Later that spring, she'd return to help Alexa pack her things and fly with her back to the States. She'd say *hi* and *bye* to Jack again, and then she and Alexa would stop in Barcelona, Monaco, and Milan on their way home.

For now, she would say her *goodbyes* then return home to New York City, which was currently receiving snow. Her loft in Brooklyn would be empty, and soon, she would no longer have an office of her own.

"Alexa, are you almost ready? I'm starving," Lindsey called out to the other room in the suite.

"I'm coming. Just a little slow this morning," Alexa said as she popped her head through the door of her room. She was still in her robe, and her wet hair was tied up in a towel.

"You're not even close to being ready," Lindsey said at the sight.

"I know. I kind of overslept. I just wanted to experience that squishy bed for as long as I could. Dorm beds are terrible—French or not." Alexa smiled.

Lindsey couldn't argue with that. "It's fine. Take your time. I'm going to go down and get some coffee and a croissant. I'll order you that muesli you liked."

"Thanks, Mom. I'll be down in fifteen," she shouted from her room.

"See you then." Lindsey sat on the bed and pulled her leather boots over her jeans and zipped them up.

Downstairs, the dining area already bustled with people ready to start their day. Many had arrived the night before and were making plans to see all the sights. Lindsey meandered past the tables at the entrance and was about to find her own when she saw Kathryn sitting alone.

Kathryn looked up as Lindsey approached. "I was hoping to see you before I left," Kathryn said. Without prompting, Lindsey pulled back the chair next to Kathryn and took a seat. Kathryn then produced a white handkerchief from her purse. Lindsey looked at its worn edges and wondered if it had belonged to Kathryn's late husband. Kathryn unwrapped the white cloth to reveal a lock. "Look," she said as she handed it to Lindsey.

Lindsey gasped with delight. She understood what it was immediately. "You found it."

"Hugo did," Kathryn said as Lindsey held the delicate lock in her hands and read the inscription. "After the show, he went back with a flashlight and searched for hours."

"I'm so glad." Lindsey handed the lock back to Kathryn.

Kathryn held it in her hands and looked at it once more, tracing and retracing the engraved names with her pointer finger. "You know, I thought I'd be sad seeing it again.

But it's just the opposite. It reminds me of how happy James and I were on that bridge." She tucked the lock back into the handkerchief, then looked at Lindsey with a smile on her face. "I found something I thought was lost forever. Hope."

Lindsey took this in.

"He was the love of my life. And I know he'd want me to find love again."

Lindsey placed her hand gently on Kathryn's forearm, reassuring her. "I'm sure he would."

But Kathryn wasn't done. "And you should, too, my dear." They both paused as Lindsey let that settle in.

Across the way, Trent was at the door on his cell phone. Kathryn nodded to him. "Is he what you're looking for? Or is he just an excuse to avoid what's really in your heart?"

Lindsey looked at Trent, then back at Kathryn. "I'm not sure what you mean."

"I think you do," Kathryn said.

Lindsey looked down at her coffee. She didn't know what to say. Kathryn was right, but what could she do about it?

"My goodness, listen to me," Kathryn said, shaking her head. She placed her hands on top of the lock. "One rusted lock, and I'm giving out advice. It just goes by so quickly."

"Paris?"

Kathryn shook her head. "Life."

Kathryn and Lindsey locked eyes, and Lindsey knew they both understood the gravity of that statement all too well.

Alexa came into the room. She passed by Trent, who was still on the phone, and waved hello. Then she walked straight over to Kathryn and Lindsey's table.

"Hi," Alexa said with a bright smile on her face and her arms wide open. "I just wanted to say goodbye," she said as she gave Kathryn a big hug.

"I have a feeling you'll be seeing a lot more of her here," Lindsey said as Alexa pulled away and stood upright.

Lindsey and Kathryn exchanged a knowing smile. "Yes, well, it's just a train ride away, and I do love the train," Kathryn said. Alexa giggled. "When I come back, I'd love to see all your new paintings."

Alexa placed her hand on the back of Kathryn's chair. "I'll give you a private showing."

"Brilliant," Kathryn said, then turned to Lindsey. "And when do you leave?"

Lindsey gave a small shudder. "Tonight." Saying it out loud made her departure real.

"Well, you'll have to let me know how it all turns out," Kathryn said.

"Oh, I'm sure Hugo will be giving you

every last detail." Lindsey smiled at the thought.

"I'm counting on it," Kathryn laughed, then squeezed Alexa's hand. "It's been so great meeting you both."

"You as well," Lindsey said.

"Please let me know when you're back," Alexa said as Kathryn got up to leave. "I'd love to show you my work."

"I'm sure you'll know when I return. That Hugo can't keep a secret." Kathryn gathered the lock and placed it in her purse. The women all laughed and said their goodbyes. Alexa then joined Lindsey at the table. As they ate their breakfast, they planned their day. A walk along the Seine, packing, then moving Alexa into her dorm.

Trent stopped by their table to say good bye, as well. "I'll see you in New York," he told Lindsey, then turned to Alexa. "And you, enjoy Paris."

"I will."

"See you in New York," Lindsey said as Trent left.

After breakfast, Lindsey and Alexa put on their jackets and exited out into the Paris winter sun. They walked down the cobblestone way outside the hotel, across the street, and over to the walkway along the Seine, approaching the Pont Neuf.

"I'm so glad we're doing this," Alexa exclaimed as she took a deep breath.

"One last walk," Lindsey said as they made their way along the river.

"Don't say 'one last walk.'"

"Did I say 'last?' I meant 'the first walk of the last day,'" Lindsey said.

Alexa laughed. "You've come a long way, Mom."

"*We've* come a long way," Lindsey corrected her.

Alexa nodded. "Yes, we have."

They continued walking along the bridge, passing by a smattering of locks attached to some of the sculptured areas. "Oh, look at all this love." Alexa placed her hand on the locks as they walked by. She stopped at an outcropping of seven locks all held together on a chain over the hand of a cherub sculpture. "I wonder how many of these people are actually still together?" She ran her fingers over each one.

Lindsey looked out at the water below and then the locks. "All of them," she said. "In some way."

Alexa smiled. "That's not what you said last time."

Lindsey nodded and crossed her arms across her chest to warm her body. "Well, maybe I'm a little less *un*romantic than I thought."

"Less unromantic," Alexa said with a curious look. "Double negative. You do realize that means... romantic."

Lindsey stepped forward and placed her hands on Alexa's shoulders. It was a typical mom moment, only Alexa wasn't being scolded. "You're supposed to fall in love in Paris," Lindsey said. "I want you to enjoy these next few months."

Alexa laughed. "I think Paris has changed you, Mom."

Lindsey laughed. "I don't know what you're talking about. But we do still have a few more parts of the city to see before I leave."

"Yes, we do," Alexa said. "Okay, let's hit the Louvre. Then, um, we'll take a selfie at the clock tower at the Sorbonne. Unless you did that last time you were here."

"Selfies?" Lindsey proclaimed as she pulled the hair away from her face. "We didn't have selfies. We didn't have phones."

"You're old." Alexa giggled. Lindsey put her arm around her daughter and laughed. They took a selfie on the bridge, then continued their walk through the city.

After several hours of exploring, they made their way back to the hotel. Lindsey helped Alexa pack her bags. She even shoved the extra free toiletries from the hotel in there. Alexa laughed. "Mom, I think I can buy soap in France. And, if not, I'm sure I can come back and ask Jack for some."

"I know, I just don't want you to have to worry."

"Mom, I've already been in school a semester. If you did this when you were my age, then I can do this," Alexa said, zipping up her bag.

"You're right," Lindsey relented and wondered if the worry instinct ever went away for moms. "Are you ready?"

"Absolutely." Alexa threw her backpack over her shoulders and placed her bags upright. "Let's do this."

J.P. met them at Alexa's dorm. He'd told them that the elevator there was tricky and they might have to carry Alexa's bags to her room, so he'd offered to help.

They stood at the bottom of the grand staircase that led up to the dorm rooms. Lindsey shifted her weight from foot to foot in a nervous manner.

"Don't worry, I'll be with her every day," J.P. said.

"Not helping, J.P.," Lindsey replied. She had certainly become less unromantic, but she still didn't want to see her daughter's heart get broken.

"I mean, I'll look after her," J.P. explained.

"Thank you," Lindsey said. "That means a lot to me."

J.P. smiled, then looked at them both. "I'll leave you two to say goodbye." He took a step toward Lindsey, then double-kissed her cheeks. "Bon voyage."

Lindsey smiled. "Thank you."

J.P. picked up Alexa's bags and began walking up the stairs.

Once J.P. was out of earshot, Lindsey nudged Alexa with her shoulder. "I like him," she said.

"I love him," Alexa replied, then waited for her response.

"I know."

Alexa's mouth dropped. "You're not going to talk me out of it?"

Lindsey shook her head. "I couldn't anyway. And no."

"This trip has been so much fun," Alexa said. Lindsey reflected back on the past four days. It really had been an amazing trip.

"You sure you don't want me to stay and help you set up your room?" Lindsey asked, hoping for just a tiny bit more time together.

"Do I hear a helicopter?" Alexa asked, looking up.

"I'll make your bed with hospital corners," Lindsey replied, trying to sweeten the deal.

"I appreciate that," Alexa said. "But it's time for me to make my own bed."

The mother-daughter team shared a look. Alexa was a young woman now who needed to fly on her own. Lindsey knew this, yet she would miss her dearly. Why did time have to move so fast? She was about to make one more plea when Alexa spoke.

"Now go. You have just enough time to say goodbye to Hugo before your flight." She reached over and hugged her mom. "I love you."

"I love you too, sweetie," Lindsey said, holding her daughter tight.

When they broke apart, Lindsey smiled, squeezed her hands, and walked off. "Talk to you tomorrow!"

"Mom," Alexa pleaded.

"Did I say tomorrow? I meant the day after," Lindsey said as she left the building. Alexa waited at the bottom of the stairs for J.P. to return but was greeted by two girls her age who were headed in her direction.

Alexa smiled and walked up the stairs with them. Her first official day at the Sorbonne was off to a great start.

Lindsey made her way across the campus and over to Hugo's studio. When she arrived, she let herself in. She took off her jacket and gloves, placed them on the chair at the entrance, and walked inside. She entered the main work area and looked up to see Hugo working on a painting in the loft.

"Hugo," she called to him. She walked to the ladder. "I thought you sold out," Lindsey said as she noticed a couple of paintings still hanging on the walls and dispersed on several easels.

"I always keep a few of my favorites, you know that," Hugo said as he came down the ladder.

Lindsey admired the portrait of Kathryn on display on the center easel. Hugo then pointed to an area behind her. "Look," he said. Lindsey turned to find her finished painting of the Pont des Arts on another easel.

"It's your best work," Hugo said. "So far…"

"You really do always say that." Lindsey laughed as she looked at the painting. Though it took her years to complete, she was proud of the piece.

"This time, it might even be true," Hugo said.

Lindsey looked at the painting and thought about the history behind it, both personal and impersonal. "What do you think will happen when all the locks on all the bridges come off?"

"People always find a way to show love." Hugo sighed, looking at the painting. "Art. Music. Maybe even the ineloquent words of a sappy teenager or an aging artist. Or a hotel owner."

Lindsey managed a sideways glance at Hugo. Always meddling.

"You want me to ship it to you?" Hugo asked.

"Keep it here," Lindsey said. She hadn't told Alexa about the painting, and she wanted her to find it one day when she came to paint in the studio. It was the equivalent of her writing special messages on her napkins in her lunchbox when she was a kid. She wanted her to know she was still thinking of her.

"Good, I was hoping you'd say that. I have a special place for it," he said.

"Then I'll see it when I come back." Lindsey was looking forward to that time.

"I'll count the days," Hugo said.

Lindsey put her arm around him. "Me too." He placed his arm around her and they embraced.

"I'm going to miss you, Hugo," she said.

"I know."

"Take care of my girl."

"Oh, she will do fine," Hugo said, then pointed to Lindsey's painting. "After all, you did."

Lindsey smiled and nodded. Hugo was right.

Lindsey took one last look at the painting. It may have taken her twenty years to complete it, but she had finished what she'd started. Now, she had to say her goodbyes to Jack.

Jack was working the desk, where Trent was settling his bill. "Thanks again for the upgrade," Trent said.

"Don't mention it," Jack replied.

"And I will be sure to recommend the hotel to all of my associates," Trent said, signing the bill.

"And we'll be sure to put all your magazines in our lobby," Jack said, pointing at the small entranceway.

"Oh, you'll need a bigger lobby for that," Trent said.

Jack shared a knowing look with the other man, then reached out his hand. "Hey, good luck with everything."

Trent shook his hand. "Thanks. You too."

Trent's phone rang. He let go of Jack's hand and answered. "Hello?—Yep." As he picked up his briefcase, he stood to find himself face-to-face with Lindsey. "Hold on one second," he said to the caller.

"There she is," Trent said to Lindsey. "I'll see you back in New York." He double-kissed her goodbye.

"Great. I'll see you then," Lindsey said.

As Lindsey watched Trent leave, she wondered what their next meeting would be like. Jack walked around the counter and stood in front of her rubbing his hands together, a nervous habit Lindsey knew he'd had since college.

"So, this is it, I guess," Lindsey said.

"Yeah, I guess it is." Jack leaned back over the desk. "Lindsey, I got you a little something before you go."

He pulled out a sketch and unrolled it for her to see. She gasped in surprise. It was the portrait they'd had done in the park years ago. "I've held on to it long enough, and now it's your turn," Jack said as he handed it to her.

"You kept it?" She figured that when Jack had never shown up, he had tossed all memories of her, but the sketch proved her wrong.

"I always thought it'd be worth something someday," Jack said. Lindsey smiled. There was a long pause between them, then Jack began. "Um, listen, Lindsey, I just wanted to say that I'm in—"

Before Jack could finish, a voice called through the door. "Jack."

Lindsey and Jack turned to see Nicole.

Nicole walked between Jack and Lindsey

and linked her arm in Jack's. "I heard you were leaving."

"Yes," Lindsey said. The moment had been interrupted. Her spirit slumped in defeat. She began gathering up her things.

"Do come back and visit us someday," Nicole said with a fake smile.

"I will." There was another moment of silence, then it was Lindsey's turn to speak, but all she could muster was, "Goodbye, Jack."

"Goodbye, Lindsey," Jack said. There was no hug. No hint of anything special. Lindsey walked away and out the door with her head hung low.

Snow was beginning to fall outside. Lindsey got in her taxi and shut the door. She took one last look at the hotel and saw Jack peering at her from the window. The taxi moved into the drive and inched away. Lindsey continued to look at Jack, wondering if, this time, he'd have the guts to follow her. But her taxi took off down the cobblestone street, and no one reached out to stop the car.

She left Paris, once again leaving Jack behind.

Chapter Fourteen

The Time and the Place is Now

THE NEXT MORNING, LINDSEY WOKE to find the entire city coated in six inches of fresh powder. The winter storm had hit hard the previous night, just as her plane landed in New York. When she'd finally made it back to her townhome in Brooklyn, there was already two inches of snow on the ground.

She'd taken a shower, made a cup of tea, and curled up in bed to read a book. She'd read only three pages when she fell fast asleep. Eight hours later, she woke in a start just as the sun began to peek through the windows. She'd been in such a daze that she'd called out to Alexa to see if she was awake. When there was no response, she realized she was no longer in Paris, but back home in New York.

She dressed for the day in her cozy red cashmere sweater, then made her way downstairs, passing by Alexa's empty room.

She was back to being an empty nester, and the view of the gray skyline of Manhattan, though stunning, didn't make her feel any better.

Once downstairs, Lindsey opened the front door and scooped up the snow-covered *New York Times*. She made her way back to the kitchen and filled her French press with grounds she had bought on the way out of Paris. As she waited for the coffee to brew, she opened the paper and found the crossword puzzle. She grabbed a pen and went to work.

"Five letter word for Valentine," she mumbled, then shrugged her shoulders.

Contemplating the answer, she looked over to the kitchen and saw two small pieces of dried spaghetti stuck to the whitewashed brick wall. She smiled at the memory of the last meal she and Alexa had cooked there and decided to leave the pasta on the wall.

She wondered what Jack was doing in Paris. Maybe he was sitting at his hotel bar, doing his own crossword puzzle. Did he regret not running after her? Or at least, not leaving without a proper goodbye? Would they go another twenty years—or more—without seeing each other again?

He was probably working the bar that night and assuring his guests were well taken care of. As she sipped her coffee, Lindsey wished that she was sitting there instead, with a glass of wine… but that was a fruitless thought. She couldn't sit at his bar for the rest of her life, waiting for Jack to make a decision or a commitment. Besides, she had bigger worries.

She had to prepare the magazine for the buyout and ensure that everyone was going to be fine. While she'd sent a companywide email announcing the sale, she had yet to talk to everyone in person, and she wanted to make sure that her team understood that she wasn't abandoning them. Her original plan had been to stay on and consult, but when she woke up that morning, she realized that if she stayed with the magazine, she really wouldn't be moving on and embracing the change. She had to be all in or all out.

Lindsey finished her cup of coffee, then headed downtown. The streets of Manhattan were packed with people. She felt at home, yet somehow, profoundly out of place. Once she arrived, she put on her best game face and rode the elevator up to *POV*.

The magazine offices were bustling with the daily hustle. Editors were typing, and designers were fixing layout issues and processing photos for print.

Maggie greeted Lindsey with a huge hug. "You're back!"

"I'm back," Lindsey said as she wrapped

her arms around Maggie, then handed her a shopping bag. "And I brought you chocolate and perfume."

Maggie took the bag and peeked inside. "No boyfriend?"

"Sorry," Lindsey said with a smile as she turned to wave good morning to some of her other employees.

"How's Alexa?" Maggie asked, following Lindsey to her office. "Are you sad?"

Lindsey kept walking. "Actually, I'm okay." She continued greeting her employees as she made her way down the hall.

"So there's a cure for empty-nest syndrome?" Maggie asked.

"I wouldn't say 'cure,' but there is Skype," Lindsey said, moving toward her office.

Maggie walked quickly behind Lindsey, then nervously blurted, "So, you really said yes to Trent."

Lindsey smiled. "I really did. He's coming over in a few hours so that we can discuss all the details of the sale and I can sign the paperwork. But first, I've got a million emails to catch up on."

"Absolutely," Maggie said as they approached Lindsey's office. "I'll let you get to work. And I'll be sure to let you know when Trent arrives. If you need anything else, I'll be at my desk."

"Thanks." Maggie left and shut the office

door behind her. Lindsey was going to miss her. She had been her assistant for the past three years and knew her every move before she made it. She thought about where she would find someone like Maggie again, but realized she wouldn't have to. Selling the magazine meant she would no longer have a job or a need for an assistant. Lindsey took a deep breath. Once she sold the magazine, she would have to figure out what she was going to do with all her free time. The thought frightened her. While she knew it was time to move on, and she was making a smart move, she was still fearful of the future.

Lindsey decided that today wasn't the day to think about it. Until she signed on the dotted line, *POV* was still her baby, and she needed to take care of it. Lindsey went to work answering emails. One hour later, Maggie was back at her door. "He's here," she said.

"Send him in." Lindsey put down her pen and stood up to greet Trent.

"Hey," Trent said as he entered her office. Lindsey walked around her desk, and the two embraced in an awkward hug. "So, ready for all this?" he asked.

Lindsey took a deep breath. "About that…"

Trent panicked. "Don't tell me you changed your mind."

Lindsey gave him a playful smile. "Nope. The magazine's still yours to make bigger and better." Lindsey paused, then finished with a more serious tone. "It's just... I'm not staying."

Trent was shocked. "Why? What happened?"

Lindsey stood still for a moment, then answered. "Paris, I guess." Then she divulged something that had occurred to her as she was sending out her last *POV* emails. "The truth is, I started an art magazine because I wasn't brave enough to be an artist." Lindsey stopped for a moment. "Wow, I've never admitted that." Trent nodded in a gesture that urged her to continue. "I want to paint again. And I know I might not be good enough – maybe I'll just end up with a cat, sketching people in the park – but at least I'll have tried."

Trent stood still as if he was taking it all in. "Really?" he asked. Lindsey nodded. "Are you sure about all this?"

"No. No," Lindsey said. "But I'm doing it anyway."

A look of disappointment crossed Trent's face. "So, I get the magazine but not you."

"I'm sorry," Lindsey said.

"Me too," Trent said. "I guess someone *can* say no to me."

Lindsey laughed and wondered if she

was the first woman he'd met in a long time who challenged him. "I doubt it will ever happen again."

Trent chuckled. "Yeah, we'll see." Trent grabbed his briefcase and switched to work mode quickly. He balanced his leather bag on top of the chair in front of Lindsey's desk and pulled out a stack of papers. "You should probably have your lawyers check that out," he said as he handed the documents to Lindsey. "And that will be that." Trent zipped up his bag and walked toward the door. He stood in front of Lindsey and held out his hand. Everything was business now. "Goodbye, Lindsey," he said.

"Goodbye," Lindsey said as she shook Trent's hand. He turned and left.

Lindsey would take the papers to her lawyer, and if everything was in order, she would sign them, and the magazine would no longer be hers. She leaned against her desk, feeling a twinge of wistfulness. This really was the end. For the past ten years, the magazine had been her love, and that affair was over. It was time for Lindsey to find something new, and her hope was that painting would be her new passion.

A month later, Jack had managed to move forward. Lindsey was gone. He assumed he might see her again when she came to pick up Alexa at the end of the semester, but he figured that since he hadn't heard from her, that was it.

He had immersed himself once again in his business and was busy making his morning rounds when he stopped at the front desk to check on the day's reservations and noticed the painting above it.

He knew Hugo had dropped off some of his art for the maintenance crew to hang the night before, but he didn't know what had been left behind. He had simply instructed the crew on where the pieces should go. That morning, however, Jack was completely caught off guard by this one painting.

Not because it was bad—it was the exact opposite. It was magnificent, and it wasn't Hugo's, it was Lindsey's. He had remembered the painting of the Pont des Arts bridge she had begun just weeks before she had left for New York the first time. She had been so enthusiastic about capturing the color of the setting sun but had always complained that she'd never been able to create the right shade of orange. She'd let Jack see the painting only once, but he recognized it right away. He never thought Lindsey had finished it.

Then it occurred to him. She had spent quite a bit of time at Hugo's studio when she was in Paris in January. Had she finished it then? And had she instructed Hugo to send it over? Or was Hugo meddling again?

Either way, Jack knew what he needed to do next.

He picked up the phone and called Nicole. "Can I come see you? We need to talk."

"What do we need to talk about?" Nicole asked.

Jack knew she had to think something was up. Normally, he was too busy with work to reach out to her in the middle of the day. "We need to talk about us."

"Okay," she said. "I'm at my place now. Come over."

Jack hung up the phone and headed straight to Nicole's.

In New York City, Lindsey had settled into her new routine without *POV*. She had taken the last month to relax. She woke up late and did the crossword puzzle. She walked around the city for the entire day, visiting museums and restaurants she'd never had time to go to before. She did all the things that made New York the city that it was, and she enjoyed every moment. Then she came home and painted. It was the life she had wanted when she was young, except for one small thing.

Jack had remained a distant memory,

just like he'd been before; however, that day, she couldn't get him out of her head. When she walked outside to pick up the newspaper, she was reminded that today was no ordinary day. Today was Valentine's Day. The paper had a sleeve covering it with a big advertisement for the holiday.

Lindsey opened her computer and dialed Alexa on Skype.

"Tell me you're not alone on Valentine's Day," Alexa said without even saying hello.

"Is that today?" Lindsey joked.

Alexa smiled, then excitedly told her mom, "Guess what? J.P. and I put our lock on the bridge today. It's beautiful and I don't care if they cut it off."

Lindsey grinned. "People will always find a way to show their love." Just as she said that, Lindsey looked out her window and saw a red balloon with the words "Happy Valentine's Day" float by.

Lindsey thought it was simply a delivery boy walking by with a package for her neighbor, but the balloon wasn't moving. Instead, it hung in front of her large front window. Lindsey became curious. She thought it was odd that it was so conspicuously placed in front of her home. She had to find out what was going on. "Alexa, I got to go. I think someone's here," Lindsey said.

"Like a Valentine?" Alexa teased.

"No, I'm sure it's something for the neighbor. But I'm going to go check it out."

"Okay, be careful," Alexa said.

"I will. And you have fun with J.P. tonight. I'll talk to you tomorrow. Happy Valentine's Day. I love you," Lindsey said quickly as her eyes remained focused on the balloon outside.

"I love you, too," Alexa said, then blew a kiss to her mom and hung up.

Lindsey logged out of Skype, then walked over to the big bay window that looked out to her front walkway. The balloon was gone. She saw it sitting on the porch of her neighbor's house attached to a bouquet of roses.

Lindsey laughed to herself. What was she thinking? Of course, there wasn't a Valentine's Day surprise for her. Trent was long gone, and so was Jack, and she certainly hadn't met anyone new. Lindsey turned to walk back to her crossword puzzle. *Today is just like any other day. Nothing special.*

But then, something caught her eye.

She turned further to the left. In the middle of her snow-covered side porch was a bunch of balloons tied together and weighted down by a wrapped box. *What is this?* She wondered if the delivery boy had accidentally thrown it over her fence thinking it was her neighbor's porch. She got closer to the sliding glass door so that she could look outside and see if there was a name on the card. When she could finally see the whole thing, she found that the bunch of balloons was not alone. Tied to her picnic table with a chain and a lock was—

"Jack!" Lindsey exclaimed at the sight of him locked to her outdoor furniture. She slid open the door.

Jack looked up with a joyful expression and held out a bouquet of red tulips. "Happy Valentine's Day!"

Lindsey's heart pounded in double time as she pulled the sliding door open all the way. "What are you doing here?"

"It's a grand romantic gesture gone awry," Jack said, his breath fogging in the cold.

She laughed, feeling light and giddy. He was here. He'd really come to meet her this time.

"It's freezing, get inside."

Jack wiggled his hands and managed to get himself free from the chains. He picked up the flowers and followed Lindsey inside to the warmth of her home.

"I thought you were going to notice me a lot sooner than that," Jack said, shivering.

"No one does romance like you."

"No one does romance quite like us." Jack handed her the bouquet of tulips.

"Are these business flowers?"

"These are definitely *not* business flowers." His eyes filled with adoration and regret. "Lindsey, I'm sorry."

She sighed. "Jack, you don't have to do this."

"No, listen," he said. "I do." Lindsey let him speak. "I should've followed you twenty years ago. I should have followed you weeks ago. But I'm here now, and I'm asking for another chance."

Lindsey took a deep breath. For over twenty years, she'd been waiting for this precise moment. For just a moment, she thought about giving Jack the runaround, telling him that he was too late, or telling him that he'd had his chance, but she couldn't do it.

"I think something can be arranged," Lindsey said. She didn't need to hear anything else. A bigger apology or more flowers wasn't necessary. She wanted to be with him. It was plain and simple.

Jack had finally shown up in New York, and that was all Lindsey had ever needed.

He took the flowers and placed them on the table to his left. He looked at Lindsey with a smile, then leaned in closer for a kiss. Their lips met, and right there on Valentine's Day, all the love she'd ever felt for him came rushing back again, as though it had always been there. Maybe it always had. She knew he felt it too. Her body melted in his arms.

It may not have been the top of the Empire State Building, but Lindsey would always remember their first kiss on American soil.

She pulled away from Jack and said in wonder, "I can't believe you're here."

"Of course I'm here. It just took me a little longer than we'd originally planned." Jack laughed.

"That's one way to put it," Lindsey said. "Well, I'm glad you finally made it."

Jack pulled her in and kissed her again.

For the next three hours, they cuddled up on Lindsey's couch, and Jack started a fire in her fireplace. He was finally seeing Lindsey's world, and she was happy to show it to him.

Lindsey brought out a big knit blanket, and they cozied up underneath it. They kissed and reminisced about their time together in the past, but they still hadn't addressed the future.

"What do we do now?" Lindsey asked as the last log slowly burned out.

"Well, you should probably put those flowers in water," Jack said matter-of-factly.

"Oh my gosh, yes." She had gotten so distracted by Jack that she had forgotten. After she took care of the tulips and arranged them on her dining table, she sat back on the couch with him.

"But, seriously, what's next? Are you moving to New York?" Lindsey asked.

He paused.

"I made a reservation for dinner tonight at Le Cirque," he said. "But that's as far as I got."

Lindsey couldn't help but smile. "You never were one for making plans."

"Life is what happens when you're making plans," he reminded her. "I prefer to just live life."

She sat on the couch and leaned back with a sigh. "You know what? You're right. Why make plans when we can just enjoy the moment?"

"That's exactly what I wanted to hear." He pulled her close for another kiss. "Let's enjoy tonight. We can figure out tomorrow, tomorrow."

"Deal."

For the next twenty-four hours, they made no plans, except to do what they felt. If they were hungry, they ate. If they were tired, they slept. If they wanted to laugh, they talked. If they wanted to feel loved, they embraced.

Lindsey hadn't been this carefree since she'd lived in Paris as a young woman, and she knew Jack hadn't taken this much time away from his hotel since the day it opened. Together, they explored this new version of themselves. They walked the streets of New York, they ate at all the best restaurants, and they sipped wine in the dark leather booths of the hidden treasures of the city.

One afternoon, a few days later, Lindsey and Jack were splitting a bottle of pinot noir at a cozy little café when Jack sprung an idea on her.

"We should go to the Empire State Building," he said.

"Are you serious?" Lindsey asked. "I thought we were putting the past behind us."

"We are. But I still think it would be romantic." Jack kissed her cheek.

"I suppose we can do it." Why shouldn't she enjoy that moment with him, after all this time?

"Come on. It'll be fun." He motioned to the waiter that he wanted to pay their bill.

They bundled up in their winter coats and braved the New York winter.

After a twenty-minute walk through the snow-covered streets, Jack and Lindsey boarded the elevator to the observation deck on top of the Empire State Building. One hundred and two floors later, they disembarked. They had skipped the open-air observation deck on the eighty-sixth floor because it was too cold that afternoon and headed straight to the top. From their vantage point, they could see all of Manhattan, down to Brooklyn, and across to New Jersey.

Lindsey hadn't been to the top of the building since she'd chaperoned Alexa's third-grade field trip to the iconic site.

"This is incredible." She didn't remember the view being that breathtaking. "I'm glad you made me come."

"Me too. Look." Jack pointed out toward Brooklyn. "We can almost see your place."

Lindsey stared out the window. She could make out the rough perimeter of where her home would be.

"It's crazy how little everything looks from up here. It's spectacular," she said.

They looked out at the expanse below them. "It's no Eiffel Tower, but it'll do," he said.

Lindsey playfully punched his upper arm. "It's gorgeous, and you know it."

"It's only gorgeous because you're here," he said. "In fact, you're the only reason I ever liked the Eiffel Tower."

"Are you saying you never went back there after that day you took me to the top?"

Jack shook his head. "Absolutely not."

"Wow. I always figured you'd have found someone else."

"I told you, you made it hard to ever want to woo anyone else. No one could compare to you," he said. "Which is why I never want to think about dating again."

She nodded in agreement. "Me neither. Dating's terrible. Especially as we get older. Who in their right mind wants to date anymore?"

"I'm glad you agree," Jack said.

"You are?" She turned around to face him.

"I am." He slowly lowered his left knee to the ground. Lindsey gasped and placed a hand over her mouth. Jack reached into his pocket and pulled out a small box. "Lindsey," he began. "I have one more plan for us."

"Are you serious?" Lindsey asked in shock.

He nodded. "Will you marry me?"

She teared up, unable to believe Jack was on one knee. Her heart pounded so hard she wondered if he could hear it. She'd always wanted him to show up, but she'd never thought he would propose. Yet, seeing him now, she knew it was what was supposed to happen. In that moment, it occurred to her what she had always wanted. It wasn't a grand gesture, it wasn't someone who could follow the plans; it was simply Jack. She wanted Jack in her life.

"Yes!" she exclaimed. "I'll marry you."

Jack took the diamond ring from the box and placed it on her left hand. The sky turned a deep orange and the diamond sparkled against the backdrop of the city. Lindsey wrapped her arms around Jack, and they embraced in tears.

"I can't believe this," she said as they peeled apart from one another. "Did you have this whole thing planned?"

"Of course I did," Jack said nonchalantly. "I just couldn't let you know. If you'd had a clue, you'd have tried to over-plan."

Lindsey laughed. He knew her too well.

"So the last few days you just pretended that we were living on a whim, in the moment?" Lindsey asked.

"The same way I pretended that I just happened to meet you in art history class," Jack said. "When a guy falls in love at first sight, he always has a plan."

He gently pulled her close, then kissed her passionately.

"I love you, Jack."

"I love you, too." He stood behind her and wrapped his arms around her shoulders, clasping them in front of her chest. Together, they watched the sun set. The beautiful colors seemed to reflect the emotions that swirled within her. She needed to paint this.

To capture the moment, she pulled out her phone, reversed the camera, held it out, and quickly took a selfie of the two of them. Though this afternoon would be ingrained in her memory for the rest of her life, she wanted a photo to show Alexa.

She was not unromantic anymore, and she needed proof for her daughter.

"By the way," Jack said. "I didn't know your father's number, so I asked Alexa for permission."

"You asked Alexa for permission to marry me?" Lindsey asked, surprised.

"I figured it was the right thing to do if I was going to be part of your family," Jack said. Lindsey had no words. It was one of the most thoughtful gestures she had ever experienced.

She kissed him on the lips just as the last remaining sliver of the sun disappeared over the horizon.

"Thank you," she said.

They embraced again and took in the view. The Empire State Building would forever be the place they committed to each other.

"We're getting married!" Lindsey shouted to anyone who would listen. The crowd of tourists around them applauded.

Jack laughed. "So, this is a good thing?"

"This is an amazing thing," she said. "But, Jack, do you have a plan after this?"

Jack shook his head, then smiled with a wink, and she knew he knew exactly what would happen next, but he would never let on. He was a boy with a plan to get the girl he saw and fell in love with, but he would always make it seem like chance that they ended up together.

Chapter Fifteen

A New Time, A New Place

THREE WEEKS LATER, LINDSEY WAS painting again. She had spent two hours
mixing her colors so that they matched the
sunset in Manhattan perfectly. She was
painting a cityscape slowly and meticulously,
stroke by stroke.

"Now *that's* your best work," Hugo said,
looking at Lindsey's new painting.

Lindsey shook her head at Hugo's re-
mark. "Hugo, you always say that."

After Jack had proposed, they'd decided
to rent out Lindsey's townhome and move to
Paris for the rest of the semester.

Jack had known that Alexa was home-
sick and missed her mom, and Jack missed
her, too. When he left for New York, he not
only promised Alexa that he would marry her
mom, but he also promised that he would
bring her back. When Lindsey and Jack
returned from the Empire State Building,

the first thing Lindsey did was Skype Alexa with the news. She held up her ring and exclaimed that she was getting married. Alexa was overjoyed.

"I finally get to tell Dad that you found someone," Alexa said after Lindsey had given her all the details of the proposal.

"Yes, you do." Lindsey smiled.

"And what are you doing next? Where are you going to live?" Alexa asked. "Are you coming back to Paris?"

Lindsey paused. She hadn't thought that far ahead yet. She was still getting used to the idea that she was engaged to Jack. "I don't know," Lindsey said. "But I don't see why not."

Lindsey turned to Jack. "Could we move to Paris?"

He smiled. "Well, I technically already live there. But you can absolutely move there—with me, of course."

Lindsey was ecstatic. "I guess we're moving to Paris," she said to Alexa.

Alexa squealed with delight. "Yay! I can't wait to give you a big hug. And Jack, too. See you soon!"

It didn't take long for Jack to help Lindsey pack everything she needed and rent out her townhome. Their plan from that day forward was simple.

Jack would continue running the hotel,

and Lindsey would go back to painting. The rest, they decided, they'd figure out as they went—the details of the wedding, where they'd live permanently, where Alexa would stay.

On her last day in New York, Lindsey took some time alone to say a long goodbye to her place and her past. In that moment, she realized that for someone who was so resistant to change just a few months prior, she had completely changed her entire life. Yet, she had never been happier.

Once she arrived in Paris and settled into Jack's place, Lindsey set up her own work-space in Hugo's studio. When he'd heard she was returning, he'd insisted that she come and paint with him. She couldn't refuse the offer. Everything she'd loved about Paris was becoming her new reality. She was painting again, and she had Jack and Hugo, and most importantly, her daughter.

It had been a long road to get there, but there she was.

Painting in Paris.

In the studio that day, Lindsey painted in a fury. She was lost in her work when Alexa and J.P. came out from the back. Lindsey looked up and smiled at them.

"We're heading back to campus. Do you want to grab lunch first?" Alexa asked.

"Thanks, sweetie, but I think I'm going

to stay and finish this," Lindsey said, moving her brush across the canvas.

J.P. and Alexa walked around to get a glimpse of Lindsey's latest work. "It's beautiful, madame," J.P. said.

"Thanks," Lindsey replied. "I'll see you Monday?" Though she had been eager to be closer to Alexa, Lindsey had also recognized that Alexa needed space to be an adult on her own. She had vowed to become less helicopter-like and gave her daughter room to do her own thing. However, they saw each other daily in Hugo's studio, and once a week, they all went dancing.

Alexa and J.P. nodded. "Tango Monday," Alexa said. "We'll see you there." She and J.P. left hand in hand, leaving Lindsey to her work.

"Young love. Nothing like it," Hugo said, watching them leave. "Nothing like it except old love."

Lindsey smiled and pointed her brush at Hugo. "That's true." Old love was now something she knew well.

Hugo stood up from his stool. "Will you close up for me? I have to meet Kathryn for tea."

"Tea?" She'd never heard Hugo talk about drinking tea in his life.

"She's having tea. I'm having everything but," Hugo said, putting on his coat. Kathryn still lived in London but took the train to Paris nearly every weekend to visit Hugo. It was a standing invite, and at the end of every week, she showed up excitedly. Lindsey had noticed that having Kathryn in his life made Hugo's art more inspired, and though he spent less time in the studio, he was also more prolific.

Love made him efficient. Her too.

Hugo took a closer look at Lindsey's painting, then said, "More red on the bridge."

Lindsey nodded and Hugo left. Then she got back to work on her new version of the Pont des Arts bridge. This version featured a happy couple riding bikes. The inspiration for the painting was her relationship with Jack. Her intent was to meld their two worlds and their most unforgettable moments together into one painting. The background was the sunset in Manhattan from their engagement, the setting was the love locks bridge where they had sealed their fate, and the bikes served as a reminder that life is just one long ride and you have to be willing to keep pedaling. If you stop, you'll never know how it all could've turned out.

Lindsey added more red to the bridge, then took a step back from the painting. Though Hugo always said her latest work was her best work, she believed him this time. In her heart, she truly knew this was her best painting. She had spent too many years holding back her emotions, not painting everything she felt, standing on the sidelines, looking in at her life. The one time she had had the courage to put herself out there, the lock had fallen in the water and she'd been devastated. But now she had the courage to be honest in her work. She didn't know if it was age that gave her the confidence or the fact that Jack was in her life for good this time, but she felt empowered by the freedom this newfound confidence gave her.

Lindsey worked on her painting for a few more hours, then cleaned up her work area. It was a Friday afternoon and she had plans. They were the same standing plans she'd had when she was a student.

A bike ride through the city with Jack.

When she finished putting away her paints and locking up the studio, Lindsey met up with Jack at the hotel. He'd prepared two bikes for them for the day, just like he had when they were both in school.

They rode all around the city, taking in the familiar sights. The Eiffel Tower, the Louvre, Notre Dame. Lindsey was happy to be living in Paris once again. She had everything she wanted and more.

They wove through the city until they finally made their way to the Pont des Arts bridge.

"This looks familiar," Lindsey said as she dismounted her bike.

"Yes, it does," Jack said as he leaned his bike against the bridge.

"Shall we try this again?" Lindsey asked as she looped her arm through Jack's.

Jack nodded, then added, "And this time, I brought extra locks." Jack held up a red padlock with his right hand in front of Lindsey with a smile.

"How many?" Lindsey asked.

"Lots," Jack said as he pulled out two other locks with his left hand.

"Good," Lindsey said. Though they were engaged, she still had wanted to put a lock on the bridge. It was the one unresolved piece of their history.

"All right. This is it," Jack said as he produced a marker.

"Any last words?" Lindsey asked.

"Just those three," Jack replied.

Lindsey thought for a second then joked, "Ooh la la."

"Um, no," Jack said. "I was thinking of 'I love you.'"

Her cheeks warmed. "I love you, too," she said.

Lindsey held the lock out over the railing. Jack reached out and grabbed her hand, and together, they released the lock into the river. They knew all locks placed on the bridge would be cut down, but a lock in the river would weather over time—just as their first one did.

"Well, it may have taken us a while," Lindsey said.

Jack placed his hands on her shoulders and moved them down her arms. "But we got here," he said.

"We did." They inched closer and closer until there was no longer space between them. Their lips touched gently then moved together in rhythm.

They were back to a time and a place. Now. Paris. Forever.

Epilogue

A LOVE STORY NEVER TRULY ENDS. It twists and turns, soars high and crashes. It jumps tracks from one to the next, turns left then right, perpetually remaining in motion. With love, there will always be a past and a future. It is never-ending. The cycle repeats over and over, constantly marking a new time, a new place.

That is where this story continues.

The small church on the Seine reminded Lindsey of a Monet painting she had studied at the Sorbonne—*The Church and the Seine at Vetheuil*. Though the image was simplistic, the sky a hazy blue-gray, the landscape around the water that led to the place of worship was a vibrant green and full of life. Watching Hugo and Kathryn emerge from the church hand in hand, she felt that same energy she had felt the first time she'd laid eyes on the Monet. The newlyweds were buzzing with joy. Kathryn's short ivory dress with long sleeves matched the feathered fascinator upon her head. Hugo's black tux was perfectly tailored. The late summer sun shone bright overhead.

Lindsey and Jack stood with Alexa and J.P., tossing birdseed at the happy couple.

Over the past seven months, Kathryn's weekend visits to Paris had been extending longer and longer until she was spending more time in France than she was in London. Hugo had welcomed her into his life with open arms, and when he proposed, she ecstatically said yes. She had learned that life was too short to hesitate. She had found great love with James and never expected to find love again. With Hugo, life was easy. He would never replace James; he would simply be a new *amour*. He would be her second chance at happiness, and they would go on to create their own memories together.

Hugo gently escorted Kathryn down the slate stairs outside the church to the horse and carriage waiting to take them away.

"Thank you all for being here," Hugo said to Lindsey and the other three.

"Of course," Lindsey replied.

"We wouldn't have missed it for the world," Jack added.

Kathryn smiled from inside the carriage. "We'll see you at the hotel," she said. "Drinks on Hugo."

"You know he still doesn't have a tab, right?" Jack smiled.

Hugo hopped into the carriage and turned around to look at the four of them. "Ah, yes, but it's my wedding day. You'll make an exception?"

"Was already planning on it," Jack said.

"Then we'll see you all soon. I must go be with my bride," Hugo said, then turned to Kathryn and gracefully leaned in for a kiss.

Alexa and J.P. watched with smiles. "Love," Alexa said, "is a beautiful thing."

"Yes, it is," Lindsey replied.

Alexa smiled, then turned to Jack. "Have I mentioned how much I love the fact that you two are together now?"

"Every day." Jack kissed Lindsey as they all laughed.

After her semester at the Sorbonne, Alexa had stayed in France to continue painting under Hugo's tutelage for the summer. In a few weeks, she would return home to New York to see her father, then she would be back at the University of Connecticut.

"I'm going to miss you all," Alexa said.

"We'll be back in New York before you even notice we're not there," Lindsey replied. She and Jack had made plans to return to the States right before Thanksgiving. They would live in Lindsey's place for the next four months and get married that Valentine's Day in a small ceremony on top of the Empire State Building. Then, at the end of March, when the seasons began to change, they would return to France to live for the remainder of the summer. Alexa would again join them so that she could continue to paint, and they would continue this pattern of splitting time between France and the U.S. indefinitely.

"We should get back, no?" J.P. asked. "They will be waiting for us, and I planned a surprise."

Lindsey and Jack shared a look. "A surprise?" they asked in unison.

"Don't worry, it's not about your daughter," J.P. began. "I love her, but we're too young to marry."

"Oh, thank God," Lindsey said.

"Ohmygosh! Mom! Is that what you really thought?" Alexa asked.

"Well, you two have been together awhile now, and you did put your lock on the bridge," Lindsey explained.

"I haven't even finished school," Alexa exclaimed. "And the lock got cut off. Not that that means anything, but..."

"You're not making plans," Jack said.

"Exactly," Alexa said. "Mom, you need to relax more like Jack."

"I'll keep that in mind," Lindsey replied as J.P. hailed a cab.

The ride back to Jack's hotel to celebrate with Hugo and Kathryn was full of laughter. Alexa asked Jack and Lindsey to share the story of when they first met, and she couldn't get over the fact that Jack had fallen for her snot-nosed mom.

"I wasn't snot-nosed," Lindsey said. "It was allergies."

"I've seen you with allergies," Alexa replied. "It's not pretty."

"Alexa!" Lindsey exclaimed.

Alexa shrugged her shoulders. Lindsey shook her head and was about to say more when the taxi pulled up in front of the hotel. The two men exited first and opened the doors for the ladies.

Hugo and Kathryn's carriage pulled in behind them. J.P. excused himself and ran ahead.

"He's off in a hurry," Hugo said.

"He has something prepared for you," Jack said.

"He didn't paint us a painting, did he?" Hugo asked with a laugh, then turned to Alexa. "Because I saw what happened the day you tried to teach him."

"Gosh, no," Alexa said. "He's a terrible artist... but I love him."

Hugo placed his hand on Alexa's shoulder. "And that's all that matters."

Alexa smiled, and Hugo helped Kathryn

out of the carriage. The five stood outside the hotel, taking photos of the couple and each other. At one point, Lindsey and Alexa both looked up and took a picture of the sky.

"Like mother, like daughter," Jack said, watching them move in synchronicity.

The mother-daughter team laughed. "It's the only way to get the perfect color," Alexa said.

"I have taught you well, young madame," Hugo said.

"Yes, you have," Alexa replied with a smile.

They continued to take more photos until J.P. popped his head out the front door.

"Are you coming?" J.P. motioned for everyone to come inside.

The group said yes, then followed J.P. into the hotel and straight to the outdoor courtyard where he and Alexa had shared a latte on her first night in Paris.

The courtyard lights were beginning to twinkle in the afternoon sun. There was a table with a small wedding cake in the corner and a few tables dispersed around it. The space around the fountain in the middle of the courtyard had been cleared for a dance floor. Off to one side, along a brick wall, was a metal trellis.

J.P. led them directly to it. The trellis was attached to the wall and seemed out of place.

It went from the ground all the way to the roof and nearly covered the entire wall.

"What is this?" Kathryn asked.

"This is my surprise," J.P. said.

"A metal gate? It's beautiful," Hugo hesitated.

"No. No. What you see is not everything," J.P. said.

Out of the corner of her eye, Lindsey caught Jack smiling. Whatever J.P. was up to, he was in on it.

"These are the surprise," J.P. said as he pulled three brass locks from his pocket and held them up proudly.

"You brought locks?" Alexa asked. "But they cut them all off the bridges. And no one can attach any more."

"That is true," J.P. explained. "And that is why Jack and I built this."

Lindsey, Alexa, and Kathryn looked at the trellis closer. It was nearly identical to the metal gates on the Pont des Arts and Pont Neuf bridges. Now, the metal trellis made sense.

"We brought the bridge here," Jack said.

"This is amazing!" Alexa exclaimed as she threw her arms around J.P.

Lindsey looked at Jack. "You don't give up, do you?"

Jack shook his head. "Hey, at least

there's no water here. Our lock is going on this 'bridge' and it's staying."

"Ours, too?" Kathryn asked Hugo.

"Absolutely," Hugo replied. "And the best part is we will never have trouble finding it."

The three couples took their locks and wrote their names on the sides. Each then took their turn to fasten them to the trellis.

When they had finished, they all tossed their keys into the fountain in the center of the courtyard.

"Thank you for this," Hugo said to J.P.

"You're welcome. But I had a little help," J.P. said as he nodded to Jack.

Lindsey glanced at Jack. He shrugged. "Don't look at me. It was all his idea. I just made it happen."

Lindsey smiled. She didn't quite buy it, but she didn't care. Their fate had finally been sealed. She wrapped her arms around Jack and whispered, "I love you."

Jack smiled and whispered it back. "I love you, too."

As they pulled back from their embrace, a waiter approached with a bottle of champagne and six glasses. Jack helped him fill each glass and J.P. distributed them.

"Let's toast," Hugo said. "To my beautiful bride."

"And my loving husband," Kathryn said.

"To friendships that last a lifetime," Jack added.

"And art that captures it all," Alexa said.

"To a happy marriage," J.P. added.

"To the City of Love!" Lindsey said.

They held their glasses high and clinked them together. Lindsey and Alexa looked up, then locked eyes and shared a knowing look. They both saw the same thing.

In the reflection of the glasses were the three love locks...

Locked and sealed forever.

The End

French Potato Salad with Haricot Verts

A Hallmark Original Recipe

In *Love Locks*, Lindsey treasures the memories of bicycling through Paris with Jack and stopping for a picnic. Their romance rekindles when, over twenty years later, they do this again.

Yield: 8 servings
Prep Time: 10 minutes
Cook Time: 15 minutes
Total Time: 25 minutes

INGREDIENTS

- 1½ pounds baby Yukon gold potatoes, skin-on, quartered
- as needed, kosher salt
- ½ pound haricot verts (thin French green beans), trimmed
- 4 tablespoons white wine vinegar
- 1 tablespoon country Dijon mustard
- ½ teaspoon kosher salt
- ½ teaspoon black pepper
- 6 tablespoons olive oil
- 1 small red onion, thin sliced
- 2 tablespoons capers, drained
- 2 tablespoons fresh chopped Italian parsley

DIRECTIONS

1. Cook potatoes in boiling salted water for 10 to 12 minutes, or until just tender (do not overcook). Drain thoroughly.
2. Steam green beans in boiling water for 3 to 4 minutes, or until tender-crisp. Drain and immediately plunge into ice water to stop cooking process. Drain thoroughly.
3. In a large bowl, combine white wine vinegar, country Dijon mustard, salt and black pepper; slowly whisk in olive oil. Add red onion, capers and parsley; stir to blend. Add warm

potatoes and green beans and gently toss to blend. Taste and adjust seasonings.

4. Serve at room temperature. If preparing ahead, remove from refrigerator 10 minutes before serving and then gently toss to blend.

Optional: This French potato salad is delicious paired with a warm crusty baguette layered with brie cheese, French ham and fresh spring greens for a Paris picnic basket.

Thanks so much for reading *Love Locks*!

You might also like these other
books from Hallmark Publishing:

In Other Words, Love
Love on Location
Love By Chance
The Secret Ingredient
Moonlight in Vermont
A Dash of Love

For information about our new releases
and exclusive offers, sign up for our free
newsletter at hallmarkchannel.com/
hallmark-publishing-newsletter

You can also connect with us here:

Facebook.com/HallmarkPublishing

Twitter.com/HallmarkPublish